BALLET

SCHOOL

Peter and the Wolf

SCRIBO
a SALARIYA *imprint*

Published in Great Britain in MMXVII by
Scribblers, an imprint of
The Salariya Book Company Ltd
25 Marlborough Place,
Brighton BN1 1UB
www.salariya.com

© The Salariya Book Company Ltd
MMXVII

PB ISBN: 978-1-911242-84-0

1 3 5 7 9 8 6 4 2

A CIP catalogue record for this book
is available from the British Library.

Printed and bound in China.

Visit
www.salariya.com
for our online catalogue and
free fun stuff.

BALLET

SCHOOL

Peter and the Wolf

Written by
Fiona Macdonald

Illustrated by
Annaliese Stoney

SCRIBO
a SALARIYA imprint

Introduction

Rosewood Ballet School

Hi! I'm Willow—Willow Emily Maria Johnson, if you really want to know—and I'm nine years old. I live in a small messy house in a big busy city with my mom and my dad and my kid brother Jake. Mom often jokes that Dad's racing bikes live with us too; Dad's crazy about cycling and is always bringing bits of his machines indoors to clean and repair. Mom's always very busy and sometimes rather tired. She's kind and smart and studying to be a nurse. There are heaps of medical books and papers all over the house. Jake's OK really, though he teases me too much and his pet spiders are scary; I hate them! My very best friend in the whole world is Samira. She's the same age as me and she lives next door and we go to school together.

And me? I'm small and mousy-haired and quiet-looking, although Mom says I can make an awful lot of noise for my size. I quite like ordinary school—but I'm passionate about ballet. I dream of being a ballerina, but I don't know if I'll ever be good enough. I practice every day and go to ballet classes twice a week at Rosewood Ballet School. This book is about me and the school and the ballet friends I've made there.

First, let me tell you about the school. "Rosewood" sounds pretty, doesn't it? Like flowers growing among the trees. Or like the enchanted forest in Sleeping Beauty. I've watched that ballet lots of times on DVD, but I'd love to see it performed live in a theater. The story's so romantic! There's this magic scene where the Princess falls asleep for 100 years and the roses grow up and hide her ...

Sorry! I should also have said that I'm a terrible daydreamer. Well, actually, it's not terrible, it's lovely! When things get boring I just switch off and think about music and dancing. Did I say that Mom is also helping me to learn to read music and play the recorder? I'm not very good at that, but it's important for ballerinas to know about music, so I keep trying.

Anyway, back to Rosewood Ballet School. I can tell you that it's definitely not pretty to look at. There are no trees or flowers in sight. Instead, it's a big concrete building on the edge of a parking lot close to the train station. I think it used to be offices. Downstairs, there are two big ballet studios and some changing rooms; upstairs there are smaller practice rooms, a huge cupboard full of sheet music and DVDs, and several offices. Outside, it's getting very shabby. Once, the concrete was painted white, but the city air has turned that dirty gray and some of the paint is peeling.

Inside? Inside! Ah, well that's another story! To me and my ballet friends, stepping into Rosewood Ballet School is like walking into a dream factory. Once we've changed into dancing clothes and started to move in time to the music, anything seems possible. When we dance, we can be trees or flowers or birds, or kings and queens, or fairies or monsters or wizards or dragons... We can feel our bodies transforming: getting stronger, lighter on our feet, more supple, more graceful. We can leap into the air, we can twist and turn, we can let ourselves be swept along by the music and escape to a magic dancing kingdom. It's all so exciting!

Now, let me tell you about some of my ballet school friends...

Peter. There aren't many boys in our class, but Peter is one of them and he's good. He's mad about sport as well as ballet, especially soccer. Like me, he's not tall for his age—he's 10—but he's got strong muscles. He likes to have his hair cut short in a really cool style. He says he can't see to dance if it's flopping over his face; I expect he's right. He'd be very embarrassed if he heard me saying this, but I think he's got beautiful brown eyes.

Gloria. She's about the same age as me, but she's much taller. I wish I had lovely long legs like her; they make her look so elegant when she dances. Unlike me, she doesn't fidget. She's got what they call "poise." Her hair is curly brown and styled in cornrow braids. She's kind and helpful—and she plays the piano beautifully!

Jessamy. I hate to admit this, but she's the best dancer in our class. Ever so much better than me! She started ballet late, when she was almost eight, so she's older than most of us in the class. But she's learning very fast and will soon overtake us, I think, and be moved up a class to study for the next grade. She's nearly 11 now, and is working hard at school. She finds it hard to do all her homework and her ballet practice, some days. She seems rather serious at first, but is good fun when you get to know her. She's slim and delicate-looking and has curly red hair that's hard to keep neat and tidy in proper ballet fashion.

Darcey. Darcey's the only student in our class who doesn't really want to be here. Her mom has always loved ballet, and hoped to have a daughter who'd be a dancer. So, as you can see, she named Darcey after the famous ballerina, and sent her to ballet classes. But—

here's the problem—Darcey prefers the outdoor life. She's crazy about animals. She still comes to classes for now because she likes to meet her friends. She says ballet exercises help her to keep fit. She's quite right. They do!

Chapter 1
Ballet Boy & The Bullies

"**G**RRRR! SNARRRL! GROWWWWL! I'm coming to get you!..."

Mrs Josie Johnson put down her book and looked up at the kitchen ceiling.

CRASH! THUMP! "Eeeeeeeeeeeeeee! Owwwwwwww!"

Two sets of footsteps thundered noisily down the stairs.

Mrs Johnson got up from the table.

"Aaargh! Yowwwwww! Let me GO!"

Mrs Johnson left the kitchen, stepped neatly around two broken bicycle wheels and walked into the sitting room.

"Willow! That's enough!" she said.

Willow was sprawled on the carpet, breathless and laughing. Her pale cheeks were flushed and her long light-brown hair spread out in a tangled mess around her face and shoulders.

"Sorry, Mom!" she gasped, "but I was being a wolf! You know, like Peter in the dance we're doing. You should see him leap. It's fantastic! I was trying to jump like him. But there wasn't enough room upstairs for me to do it properly. I fell over and Jake laughed at me... so I chased him, AND I caught him!"

Willow curved her slim fingers into menacing wolf claws and made another grab at Jake, who was on the floor beside her. But he rolled out of reach and scrambled to his feet, making a rude face at his sister.

"Willow!" said Mrs Johnson. "Stop that! Just look at the state of your clothes! Your new school skirt is all creased and crumpled. Go and hang it up in your bedroom, and put on something else. Then you've got half an hour to do some homework before dinner's ready."

She turned to leave the room. "Jake, you can come and help me in the kitchen. I've had a busy day."

Upstairs again, Willow flung her skirt over the hook on the back of her bedroom door and scrambled into a pair of leggings. She took one look at her bag of schoolbooks—there were spellings to learn for a test next week—and turned away with a frown. She liked school and was usually quite good at spelling, but right now she had other things on her mind.

She switched on her tablet, and fitted her headphones over her ears. She gazed intently at the screen, waving her fingers and gently tapping her toes in time with the music. Soon, she was lost in an enchanted world of *arabesques* and *port de bras*, skilful solos and daring *pas de deux*, where just two people dance together in a show of balletic fireworks, and hold the audience spellbound.

"*Pas glissade… temps lié… grand jeté*," she muttered to herself. "How does she manage that perfect landing? So balanced, so light and elegant! If it were me, my feet would totally just thump down on the stage, I'm sure!"

Willow was still lost in a magic world of dancing when her mother came upstairs.

"Oh, Willow!" sighed Mrs Johnson, catching sight of the little figures leaping gracefully across the screen. "More ballet! I know you love dancing, but you really MUST do your schoolwork, as well. Why don't you go through your spellings? I can test you after dinner."

"*Piroutte, attitude*," murmured Willow, as the dancer on the screen twirled round and round, then came to a graceful halt with one leg raised, toe elegantly pointed, behind her….

"Are you listening to me, Willow?" asked her mom. "I mean it—your studies are important."

"But Mom," protested Willow. "I've got to learn! I've absolutely GOT to! My dance with Peter is really complicated. He's the wolf and I'm a bird fluttering around him. I have to make it look as if I'm flying!" She waved her fingers toward her mother. "I can manage the footwork," she said, leaping off the bed and doing a few nimble skipping steps. "But I still can't get the hand movements right... And it's only six weeks to the show!"

Mrs Johnson shook her head. "Sometimes I wonder if all this ballet is a good idea... And I meant what I said just now. You must learn those spellings after dinner!"

But Willow didn't hear her. In her daydream, she was still dancing, dancing, dancing...

Just a few streets away, Willow's friend Peter was also wondering whether ballet was 'a good idea'. After reaching home, breathless and shaking, he had shut himself away in his bedroom, hardly bothering to speak to his mom,

who was sewing new elastic onto one of his
old ballet shoes while watching TV. Propped
up cosily beside her, his baby brother George
gurgled and waved.

Now, all alone, Peter was slumped on
his bed, with his face turned to the wall.
Cautiously, he rubbed his shoulder. That's
where the boys had hit him. They'd waited
outside the school gates, just around the corner.
Then they'd walked down the road beside him,
slowly getting closer and closer until he was
surrounded.

"Hey, Ballet Boy!" they'd said, mockingly.
"Where's your tutu? And your tights? And your
pretty pink shoes?"

Peter's heart had beat wildly, and something
seemed to happen to his breathing, but he'd
tried to look brave.

The bullies jeered: "Go on, do a dance! Give
us a twirl!"

Then they'd got hold of him by the shoulders

and twisted him round and round. They'd
kicked at his feet, and tried to trip him up.
When Peter had fought back, they had started
to punch him. But he'd managed to break free
and had run like the wind. They had chased
him, of course, but could not keep up.

"At least ballet keeps me fit," thought Peter,
grimly, as he reached the safety of his back
door. Although his legs were tired after his
terrified dash to reach home, his mind was
racing, and his thoughts were in a whirl.

Peter loved dancing, and music, and learning
new steps. He loved dressing up and pretending
to be someone else on stage: a handsome prince
or an ugly frog—or anything, really. He didn't
even mind practicing the same old movements
day after day.

Sometimes he even thought he might get
quite good, if he kept on practicing. But maybe
he should just stop? Give up ballet—right now,
forever. Would that be the best thing to do? If

he gave up dancing, would the bullies leave him alone?

He sniffed, and wiped his nose on his sleeve. "It's been going on for months and months," he muttered despairingly. "I hate it. I HATE it!" He sniffed again, and slammed his fist into the bedclothes. "But I don't know how to stop them!"

With a shaky sigh, Peter hauled himself off the bed, forced himself to stand up straight, arranged his feet in the first position—toes turned out, heels touching—and took firm hold of the back of his bedroom chair. Slowly, carefully, counting the beat, he began his everyday ballet exercises. He knew—or at least he hoped—that they would help him forget the bullies for a while.

Taking a deep breath, he began: *plié, plié... battement tendu... relevé, relevé...* Over and over again. In different positions. *Devant* and *derrière*, forward and backward. Up and down. On and on.

Plié

Relevé

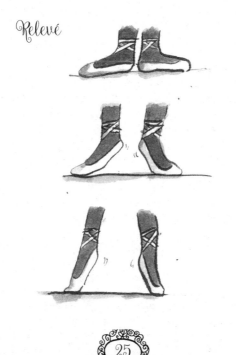

The next day, at school, it happened again. The team was competing in the junior soccer league, and Peter had been picked to play. He wasn't a member of the first team yet, though he was often one of the reserves. Only last week, Mr Jones, their sports teacher, had called him "very promising."

Peter whispered the words like a magic spell as he went to collect his sports bag from the changing room. He pulled out his shorts and his school soccer shirt, and put them on with a little glow of pride. For a moment, he felt like a proper member of the team!

But then—what was this, at the bottom of his bag? His stomach heaved and he felt suddenly sick as his fingers touched something wet and slimy and revolting.

Taking a deep breath to calm his nerves, Peter forced himself to look inside the bag. It was his boots! His soccer boots! Someone had covered them with bright pink paint. It was still wet and runny. Tucked inside was a scribbled note. There were just two words: "Ballet Boy."

Of course, Mr Jones was furious. He found Peter some spare boots to wear, and washed the pink painted boots in the showers, along with Peter's sports bag. "They'll be fine when they're dry," he promised. And they were.

But Peter wasn't.

"That was a mean trick," said Mr Jones, as they talked together after the match. "Are you sure you don't know who did it? They must have taken paint and brushes from Miss Green's art cupboard."

Peter shook his head, fighting back the tears. Words wouldn't come. He was far too frightened to name the boys who were bullying him. And anyway, he wasn't absolutely, completely sure who had painted his boots.

He thought he knew, but that made things even worse. Because... the chief suspect was one of the soccer team's best players!

Mr Jones was still talking. "If this happens again, you must tell me at once, or speak to one of the other teachers. We won't have bullying in this school! We'll do all we can to stop it!"

When Peter got home that evening, he was far too miserable to eat his dinner.

"What's the matter, Pete?" asked his dad, spearing a piece of potato on his fork. "Not hungry tonight? You're usually starving after soccer!"

"I don't want anything..." said Peter, gloomily.

"Are you sure you're OK?" asked his mom. "You don't feel sick, do you?"

"Just leave me alone!" cried Peter.

He got up from the table and ran out of the room, banging the door behind him.

Chapter 2
Two
Left Feet

It was late afternoon on a Friday, time for the Grade 3 class at Rosewood Ballet School. Until the bullying began, Peter would have said that Fridays were the best day of the week. He used to really look forward to them.

But now—well, now he didn't know what to think. When he remembered how it felt to be dancing, his spirits soared and he was full of energy, powerful and free. But when he remembered the bullies, he felt weak and helpless. His knees turned to water and his feet were heavy as lead. He sat in the front seat of his dad's car, hunched and gloomy.

Peter's dad stopped in the parking lot next to the ballet school. It was windy and raining. An empty potato chip bag and some tattered bits of newspaper blew across the open space in front of the car, together with a few soggy leaves.

"Remember, Pete," his dad said, "I'm working late tonight so you'll have to catch the bus home."

Peter's dad was proud of him in a vague sort of way, but he really didn't understand ballet. Kindly, he added: "I hope your fox dance goes well!"

"It's a WOLF dance, Dad!" said Peter. All at once, just for a moment, he felt like his old self again. "I'm dancing a big, bad wolf." He smiled and laughed: "Like this—with sharp teeth and big ears." He held his hands upright, close to each side of his face. "Howwwl! Howwwl! Howwwl!"

"I'm sure you'll be great," laughed his dad. "Just don't bite anyone! Har! Har!"

"Oh Dad…" groaned Peter. "Grow up!"

But his father's good humor was catching, and Peter's happy mood lasted for a few more minutes while he walked across the parking lot toward the scruffy, friendly ballet school building. The bright lights in its windows showed that classes had already begun. The earlier classes were for the very youngest boys and girls, some as young as just two or three years old.

Peter hadn't started that early. He was nearly six when he had his first ballet classes, and they hadn't been planned at all. He'd gone along with his mom and dad to watch the end of semester show at the ballet school. His big sister Jane was dancing in it—just a small part, one of many brightly-colored fish swimming in the sea.

Jane hadn't been very good, from what Peter could remember. She'd turned the wrong way in her dance and had almost fallen off the stage. She'd given up ballet soon afterward, but by then, Peter wanted to try it for himself. He'd hummed the tune of his sister's fish dance and jigged around, copying her steps. He'd hopped and skipped and bounced and twirled anywhere and everywhere; in the house, on the beach on vacation, down supermarket aisles and even in the playground at school. He'd looked at picture books about ballet in the local library, and watched his sister's old ballet DVDs.

"Well, we'll give it a try," his Mom had said at the start of the next semester. "If you're sure, really sure, that it's what you want to do."

Peter was sure, and old Madame Olga, who had founded Rosewood Ballet School many years ago, had been encouraging.

"Eef you worrk harrd, Pyoterrr," she had said in her old-style Russian accent, "You might be

good one day. Just maybe. But eets posseeble.
Now, look at me, and point your foot thees way.
No! Thees way! Leeft that heel! Aaah! Better!
Much better!"

All that was nearly five years ago. They'd
been good years. Peter had worked hard, and
he'd looked and listened and learned. But it had
not always been easy.

Ballet classes were not like school, with
friendly teachers who tried to make classes
interesting. No! Ballet teachers—Peter soon
discovered—were very strict. They demanded
obedience, and aimed for perfection. No idle
chatter was allowed in classes, and certainly no
messing about.

Ruefully, Peter thought about Mrs Williams,
who'd taught him in the Grade I classes. To
him, she'd seemed very old—her hair was

gray and her face was lined—though she still stood as straight and as graceful as any young ballerina. And, in spite of the fact that she was now rather overweight, she was still a very good dancer.

Mrs Williams most certainly did not want to hear what you thought about the new steps she was showing you. Peter had dared to comment once. Her sharp and scornful reply—"You really think you know better, young man?"—had taught him that lesson. Never again! Obviously, he concluded, ballet teachers know precisely what they want you to learn—and they expect you to learn it!

Slowly, very slowly, Peter came to understand why. Ballet skills had been passed down from teachers to their students for hundreds of years. Today's ballet teachers— even in a shabby building next to a litter-filled city parking lot on a wet Friday afternoon— still felt it was their duty to preserve this old knowledge and hand it on safely to the next generation. That was quite awesome, when you came to think about it.

Peter rarely thought about it at all, but, when he did, it sent a little shiver of excitement up and down his spine. He shivered now, as he walked up the concrete steps of Rosewood Ballet School, and pulled open the heavy wooden door. But this time it was for a very different reason. He had remembered the bullies, and began to feel wretched again.

As Peter walked though the door and into the entrance hall, he was met by a blast of hot air, bright light and noisy chatter. Notices pinned on the wall fluttered in the draft from the doorway. In between, big posters of famous ballet dancers in glamorous costumes and makeup added bright splashes of color. Outdoor coats and bags hung from pegs on the wall, or were heaped on chairs and benches. A jumble of boots and sneakers littered the floor.

Snatches of piano music wafted down the corridor leading to the main dance studio, together with a teacher's voice, calling out instructions to the dancers.

"ONE and two, and ONE and two... Now LIFT those ARMS and SKIP and HOP..."

Already moms and dads were arriving to take the little ones home. The beginners' class would soon be over, and Peter's more advanced class would begin.

Weaving past the huddles of waiting parents, Peter made his way to the back of the hall where some students of his own grade were standing. Already they had changed into their ballet clothes: deep pink leotards, short wrap-over skirts, neat ankle-length white socks. Some of the girls were still adjusting the ribbons that fastened their pale pink satin ballet shoes. Others were helping each other to tie their hair back into a neat ballet bun. A few had already started gentle warming up exercises. They lifted one foot just off the floor and made circles in the air with their toes, or sat with their legs stretched out in front of them, side by side, then pointed their toes as far down as possible, before bringing them up to point to the ceiling.

The sinking feeling in Peter's stomach eased a little at the sight of friendly faces. Over in the corner, he could see that Willow had already arrived, and was chatting to a tall and pretty young woman with an elegant Afro hairstyle, and two girls in ballet clothes. He couldn't hear what Willow was saying, but it must have been funny, because all of a sudden, the whole group burst out laughing.

Willow was restless, as always, hopping from one foot to another as if she was too full of energy simply to stand still. Gloria was next to her; although the girls were around the same age, she was already head and shoulders taller. She was a strong, dramatic dancer, and, unlike bouncy, noisy little Willow, had learned how to look poised and confident and calm.

Jessamy, the third girl in the group, was slender and nicely proportioned. Her long arms and legs, compact body, slim neck and neat, pretty head all just looked perfect for ballet. "Naturally graceful," the teachers said. Lucky her! Right now, she was struggling to pin back strands of her long, curly red hair; Gloria was helpfully offering some heavy-duty sculpting gel.

"Jess is the best dancer of us all," thought Peter. "And she's really keen, and works hard. But then," he thought bitterly, "I don't expect she has many worries to take her mind off dancing...."

The young woman spoke. "I'll be off now, Gloria. I want to get to the stores before they close and buy that net to make your costume. See you later—hope class goes well!"

She turned to leave. "Hi, Peter! How are you doing?" She gave him a beautiful smile. "How's the star of our show?"

Peter really liked Ruby, who was Gloria's big sister. In the daytime, she worked at the High Style Beauty Salon, but in the evenings and at weekends, she loved to help with costumes and makeup for the ballet school shows. With a wig and a few sticks of face paint, she could transform even the sweetest six-year-old into a horrible monster.

Before the bullying, Peter would have hoped that Ruby had something really wild planned for his Wolf costume. But now, her friendly greeting made him want to curl up and hide in a dark corner.

"Late as usual!" chorused Gloria, Willow and Jessamy, pointing mock-accusing fingers as a scruffy fair-haired girl with a book in one hand and a flustered expression dashed across the entrance hall. A pair of jeans and the long sleeves of a crossover ballet cardigan trailed from the bag she carried on her shoulder, as if they were trying to escape and run away.

"What do you mean?!" Darcey said, pretending to be surprised. "I'm right on time!" She grinned. "You all KNOW that I don't want to spend a minute more doing ballet than I absolutely have to. I wish I could send my mom to these classes in my place, so I could stay at home and read this book in peace, or take the dog for a run in the park, or something. Mom's the one who's ballet mad, not me!"

Just then, a crowd of young dance students streamed out of the studio and into the hall, followed by Miss Francisco, the Grade 3 teacher.

"Everyone here?" she asked. "Darcey! Stop chattering and hurry up." Darcey sighed and ran into the changing room. Miserably,

Peter unzipped his hoodie, then kicked off his sneakers and his baggy jogging pants. He was already wearing a close-fitting stretchy T-shirt and long cycle shorts underneath. He stuffed the joggers into his bag and slipped into his black ballet shoes. The elastic across the front of the foot made them easy to get on and off. No need to fuss with ankle ribbons, like the girls. Anyway, the way he felt right now, dancing seemed impossible. He might as well have two left feet.

Chapter 3
Saved by the Bell

Miss Francisco smiled welcomingly at the scattered groups waiting in the entrance hall, and led her students into the big, bright dance studio.

"Now!" she said, looking briskly around the room, "Are we ready to begin? *Révérence!*"

The French word rang round the studio. The girls in the class made a graceful curtsy to their teacher, while Peter and the other boys bent their heads in a dignified bow. On another day, Peter might have remembered that this was another old ballet tradition, loyally continued at Rosewood School. But he had other things on his mind.

Révérence

Usually, Peter loved the studio, with its high windows and huge mirrors completely covering one wall. But this Friday it filled him with dread. Automatically, he took his usual place at the long barre that ran the length of the room. Willow turned her head toward the mirror and her reflection showed a cheery smile. But Peter was lost in his own gloomy thoughts, and didn't notice. He still didn't know what to do. Should he give up ballet, or keep on coming to classes, and be bullied because of it?

"Let's begin!" said Miss Francisco. She led the class through the warm-up exercises that they had all come to know so well. First *pliés*, then *relevés*, then *battement tendu*, and *rond de jambe…* Peter had practiced these exercises so often that he could have done them in his sleep, but—as all the students had learned by now— he knew he had to concentrate and work hard if he was going to do them properly.

"Bend that right knee, Peter; keep that foot in line!" called Miss Francisco.

"I must keep trying," Peter said to himself fiercely, as he repeated the exercises again and again.

"And… rest!"

Miss Francisco walked gracefully across the studio and had a quiet word with Mrs Chang, who played the piano for their classes. The students let go of the barre and relaxed. Some leaned against the wall or did a few gentle stretches. Others repeated steps they had found difficult, in a quiet corner, to themselves.

Miss Francisco clapped her hands. "Everyone! Today's class will be slightly different to usual. I want to see how all your dances for the end of semester performance are coming along. You've all been practicing at home, I hope! Now we'll see how well you've been doing—and how the dances will work when we put them all together. Mrs Chang! Could you switch the music on, please, when I give the signal?"

Miss Francisco gave the class an encouraging smile. "You all know the story we're dancing: Peter and the Wolf. It's actually very simple. What makes it special is the wonderful music— and your wonderful dancing, too. Or at least that's what I hope!"

Was that a joke or a threat? Peter wondered. He felt a nervous fluttering in his stomach.

"Now," Miss Francisco continued, "Little Birds? Flowers? Are you all ready?" She looked around the studio. "And where's our Tree? Come along now. Remember! We count six bars for the introduction, and then the dancing begins. For your real live performance, the words that go with the music will be read by a student from our senior acting classes, but for now they're on this recording. Do you know who the reader is? David Bowie! Look—here he is, with a wolf headdress, on the cover of this old album."

"Cool!" said Willow, dashing forward to see.

"Mrs Chang! Music, please! Dancers! Are you ready? Let's begin scene one—Springtime Meadow!"

As the music flowed out of the loudspeakers, the little Birds swooped and fluttered, and the Flowers rose gracefully from the ground, arms arched above their heads to look like buds, then opening wide to become leaves and petals. They skipped and twirled on the spot, basking in the imaginary spring sunshine.

"*Ecarté devant* to finish, Birds!" called Miss Francisco. "Flowers! *Croisé derrière!*"

Ecarté devant

Darren, the tallest boy in the class, slow-marched to center stage and stood proud and strong as the mighty Tree. He bent from the waist from side to side, and waved his arms as if sudden cold winds were shaking the tree's leaves and branches.

"Ready, Ellie?" called Miss Francisco, and the smallest Bird skipped delicately around Darren's Tree, then fluttered back to join the others.

"And—two, three GO, Sam!" Miss Francisco continued. "Remember, Peter is an ordinary boy at the start of an extraordinary adventure—I want to see you looking happy, and excited and brave! Shoulders back, head held high, and a real spring in your step, please!"

And so the run-through continued, scene after scene. Willow was nicely light on her feet, skimming across the ground in a series of *coupés* and *pas de bourreés* as she danced the part of the brave and daring Bird that taunts the Cat and teases the Wolf.

"Not bad, Willow," said Miss Francisco, "Not bad at all! But we still need to work on those arms."

Willow nodded glumly and pulled a face. But she knew Miss Francisco was right. She must keep practicing!

Gloria was great as a funny but tragic duck—so pleased to be swimming and diving in lovely cool fresh water; so foolish to let herself be caught and eaten by the Wolf. Jessamy made a wonderful Cat—lithe and graceful, yet menacing at the same time.

"Check the position of those feet before you start," called Miss Francisco. "Get that *demi-plié* secure before you move to *cou-de-pied derrière*. Then your *pas de chat*—that lovely,

Pas de chat

springing jump—will be easier, and better balanced, too."

Molly, the best actor in the class, was very believable as Grandfather, even though she was a girl. She hunched her shoulders and shuffled across the floor, pausing to lean on her stick from time to time. Olly, Soo-Lin and Sophie were fierce, jolly Hunters in the forest. They had to dance holding branches of pretend leaves in front of their faces, to show that they were hiding in the bushes.

"Not as easy as it looks," said Olly. "Especially when three of us have to do it in time together!"

Darcey was a flower. Quite a good flower, technically speaking, but you could tell—even from the back of the studio—that her heart wasn't really in her dancing.

And Peter? What about Peter?

Peter stood waiting for the snarling tune on the French horns that announced his first appearance. He was still finding it hard to concentrate. Miss Francisco had worked out a wonderful dance for him—he must do it justice. For the first part of the dance, he was the Wolf lurking in the forest, hungry after the long winter and ready to catch and eat anything that moved—the Bird, the Cat, the Duck, young Peter, even tough old Grandfather!

Then, in a series of leaps, he was meant to spring out from the shelter of the forest trees and race across the open meadow, while the Little Birds and the Flowers would run away in terror.

Peter watched as the rest of their class performed their dances. Then the horns sounded—*Pah-Pah-Pah-Pah Paah Paah PAAAH–pah, PAAAH-Pah, PAAAAH!*... And Peter's dance began.

The first part, mostly crouching and crawling—more like gymnastics than ballet, really—went OK. "Still a bit ragged, Peter,"

said Miss Francisco. "But it's coming along!
Now, let's go on to the next section."

The French horns played the Wolf tune
again. Now the leaping dance began. Or at
least, it should have done. Peter stood in
position, carefully counting the beats until it
was time to take the first few running steps—
or, as they were called in ballet, *pas couru*.

"Two, three, NOW!" he said to himself.

He ran a few steps, and tensed his body to

Sissone

to spring—first *grand échappée*, then *sissone simple*... But then, all of a sudden, he shuddered to a halt and burst into tears.

BBBBBRRRRRRRIIIIIIIIIIIIINNNNNG!

The noise was deafening. What on earth was happening? Don't worry, everyone!" called Miss Francisco, as the students looked around, startled and wild-eyed. "They've been repairing the fire alarm upstairs, but I didn't think they'd be testing it during our class. I would have warned you otherwise!

"But that's our concentration ruined for this afternoon, I think. At least it's nearly the end of class. Back to the barre, please, everyone."

Nothing, not even a surprise fire alarm, could interrupt Miss Francisco's routine. The class worked its way through their usual cooling-down exercises, but in a rather half-hearted way.

They all made a final *révérence*.

"I'll see you all next week," said Miss

Francisco. "Keep on practicing at home! That run-though wasn't bad, but we've all got a lot more work to do."

She walked across to the barre, and waited until the rest of the class had left the studio in a noisy, chattering crowd.

"Now, Peter, would you like to talk about what happened?" Her voice was unusually gentle, but that made things worse, somehow.

"NO!" said Peter. "No! I can't!" And he ran out of the studio toward the changing rooms.

Chapter 4
I Hate Ballet!

Most of the other students had left for home by the time Peter had struggled into his everyday clothes, still fighting back the tears.

Darcey hurried away as quickly as she could. "That's enough ballet for one week," she laughed. "But don't worry! I won't let you down. I will practice my steps, and try not to make mistakes."

With her hair streaming messily behind her, she dashed out, dropping her book as she nearly collided with Ruby, who was on her way into the building.

"Ooops!" said Ruby. "Someone's in a hurry!

Class is over I see. Is Gloria on her way? Ah, here she is!"

Ruby was carrying a large package that rustled mysteriously.

"What's that?" asked Gloria.

"I bought the white net for the skirt of your costume," said Ruby, "but the store had some gray net, too. I thought I'd cut some feather shapes out of it and sew them to your skirt. When you wear it over your white leotard the shapes will flutter like real feathers. You'll look lovely!"

"You're so lucky, Gloria!" sighed Willow. "I don't have a big sister, and my mom hates sewing."

"Don't worry, Willow," said Gloria. "I'm going to help with costumes for everyone in the show. We've already made a fantastic wolf headdress for Peter." She laughed. "And a tail!"

"And Willow, I think Miss Francisco is planning some very special sleeves that look like wings for your Bird dance," said Ruby. "But it's not all glamour!" she added, with a smile. "She's also been talking about yellow card face masks, like beaks, for all the Birds, and the Duck, as well."

"Ohh NOOOO!" shrieked Willow and Gloria, together. "We'll look stupid!"

"I'll suggest face-paint instead," smiled Ruby. "That will do just fine. Leave it to me. And now..."—Ruby looked round the entrance hall— "Where's Jessamy? She's coming home with us, isn't she, Gloria? Ah! Jess! Are you ready?"

Together, the three of them trooped out into the rainy evening and climbed into Ruby's little car.

Peter stayed hiding in the boys' changing room until the others had gone. Gloomily, he pulled on his jacket. "There!" he said to himself with a sudden flash of anger, "I look just like any ordinary boy, not like some ballet freak." He put his ballet shoes away in his bag and tightened the laces on his sneakers. Now he was ready—or as ready as he would ever be—to face the outside world again.

He stepped out into the entrance hall. All his friends had gone, but the room was still crowded. Boys and girls for the senior class were arriving, together with men and women hurrying in from their work in stores and offices and factories. They were getting ready for advanced ballet classes, or for classes in jazz dance or break-dance or ballroom, or even (Peter pulled a face) old-fashioned country dancing.

Whatever style of dance they favored, Peter thought that almost anyone could see that all these people were dancers. Even in ordinary, everyday clothes, they moved strongly, freely and with confidence. They stood up straight and tall. Short and fat or thin and lanky, nearly all of them were quite graceful.

Most of the women had fashionable haircuts, but a few had scraped their hair back into a tight bun, like the girls in his ballet class. The style looked elegant, Peter thought, but rather uncomfortable. The same women also wore dramatic makeup, with dark brows, heavy liner and shadow to make their eyes look wider, blusher on their cheeks, and bright red lipstick.

The ballet-mad men were less easy to detect—and, in any case, there were far fewer of them. "It's so unfair!" thought Peter. "Ballet is just as athletic as any other sport, and just as skilful. It's not only for girls, yet so many people say it's not manly. They're wrong! Male dancers need to be really tough and strong—we have to support our partners in difficult poses on stage, and lift them high into the air. We do fantastic leaps and spins, and that needs serious muscle-power. I might be smaller than most of my classmates, but I bet I'm much stronger!"

He thought a bit more. "A ballet can last longer than a soccer match, so dancers need toughness and stamina. And, just like other sportsmen and women, if we want to be good—male or female—we have to spend hours and hours and *hours* training to improve our skills. That's hard work!"

Peter looked around the hall. Would he grow up to be like these adults who still loved coming to dancing classes? Was that possible? Did he even want it? If he didn't, then what else—good or bad—lay ahead?

Uh-oh! Peter's heart skipped a beat. Here was Miss Francisco, walking across the hall toward him. She was still in her teaching clothes—a long-sleeved leotard and black tights, with a knee-length skirt of light, floaty material over them. She had a warm shawl wrapped around her shoulders.

"Peter! I thought you'd gone home," she said. "How are you feeling now?"

She sat down on a chair close to where he was standing, and pulled her shawl more tightly around her. Her gray eyes, which could look so critical while she watched you dance, were now full of concern.

"Are you sure you don't want to talk about what happened? You're a good dancer, you know. We're very proud of you. All the teachers at Rosewood School would love to see you do well, and..."—Miss Francisco lowered her voice—"If there's anything that's worrying you, we're all here to help."

Peter looked down at the floor.

"If you don't want to say anything now," Miss Francisco continued, "then perhaps we could have a little talk before the start of next week's class? We might be able to think of something to make you feel better. I'll phone your parents and see if they can bring you in a little bit earlier than usual."

"Don't worry, Peter," she said, encouragingly. "Everything will be all right, I'm sure." She gave him a friendly smile. But Peter could see that, behind the smile, she was worried. He was one of the stars of her end of semester show. Could it go on without him?

His mind was in a whirl. So many different thoughts and feelings were rushing around in his brain. Miss Francisco had been kind. She was trying to help. She liked his dancing! But she didn't know about the bullies. She didn't know about school soccer, or how much he longed to be part of the team. She didn't know how he hated to be thought stupid or sissy or strange, and not like other boys, all because of ballet. She didn't—she couldn't—understand!

Even worse, thought Peter, what would his friends in the ballet class say if he dropped out of the show? They had all worked so hard, practicing new steps and learning their dances. They were all looking forward to appearing on stage in their wonderful costumes, and to dancing in front of their friends and families. If he walked away from the show, would they forgive him? Or would they hate him and never speak to him again? He couldn't bear that!

Peter shook his head sadly. Then suddenly, it all became too much. "You can't help!" he blurted out. "No one can! And I HATE ballet!"

Miss Francisco looked shocked at first, and then she sighed. "Go home, Peter," she said softly. "Get a good night's sleep and forget about dancing for a few days. I'll phone your parents and explain what's happened, and we'll see what they have to say."

She stood up, turned around and walked gracefully toward the ballet studio.

Chapter 5

The End of Everything?

It was still raining when Peter left the ballet school, and it was getting dark, as well. Grimly, he splashed his way across the wet parking lot, not even bothering to try to avoid the puddles. All he could think about was what he had shouted at Miss Francisco: *I hate ballet!*

What had he done? Had those three desperate words ruined everything, forever?

The words he'd shouted had felt true at the time. They hadn't been a lie. Standing there a few minutes ago, he really did feel like he hated ballet. He would always love dancing, of course—moving to the music was part of his very soul. But if going to ballet school made him different from the other boys, then he didn't want to go!

Whatever his feelings, he knew he'd been disrespectful to Miss Francisco. That was bad. She might not want to teach him anymore. Perhaps he'd be banned from classes. Peter frowned and then shrugged his shoulders. Fine, let them ban him from ballet! He'd have more time to practice his soccer!

Across the parking lot, Peter could still see lights shining from the tall ballet school windows. Snatches of music and cheerful conversation drifted across from the studios and the waiting dancers. Earlier this evening, the school had seemed friendly and welcoming, glowing like a beacon of promise in a gray, dull city. Now, it seemed distant, almost on another planet: it was no longer part of his world.

Scuffling and dragging his feet, Peter made his way toward the bus stop. It wasn't far away, but the rain was getting heavier. By the time he reached it, his head and shoulders were dripping. There was a kind of shelter next to the stop, but it leaked and its floor was covered in litter. Even so, Peter stepped eagerly inside. There was no one else waiting, so he'd probably just missed a bus.

The wind shook the bushes that formed a thick hedge separating the shelter from a scruffy patch of wasteland. A billboard announced that building work would start there soon. "Rosewood Mansions—New Luxury Apartments" was written in big fancy letters. For a moment, Peter was startled to see that the flats would have the same name as the ballet school. But then he shook his head, as if brushing away a fly. That was all in the past. Let it go! Leaning wearily against the back of the shelter, he wiped the rain from his face, and shivered. He was so tired, and just wanted to go home.

However, as Peter waited, he started to feel just a tiny bit more cheerful. Perhaps he was wrong to try to belong to two teams. The bullies were horrible, but at least they'd forced him to make a decision. But which should he choose? Ballet or soccer?

A second, more hopeful, thought flitted across his mind. The bullies might have stopped him doing ballet, but, *if* he were ever picked for the team, they'd never be able to stop him playing soccer. Mr Jones chose the players, and the bullies wouldn't be able to make *him* change his mind.

Also, Peter already had some friends on the soccer team. There was Arif, who played on the wing like he did, and big JJ in goal. If he hung out with them for a while, maybe the bullies would leave him alone.

And, of course, he had other good mates at school. There was Billy from down the road, and Wiktor and Zac who sat next to him in classes.

And Hannah and Sam at the school music club. But he didn't know how any of them would feel—or what they'd do—if they found out that he'd been bullied.

With a pang of regret, he thought about lively Willow and tall Gloria and messy Darcey, and the fun they all had together at Rosewood Ballet School. Soccer was great—it was his sporting passion—but he'd still miss ballet. But if giving up ballet meant he would get rid of the bullies, then that's what he would have to do. In fact, he just had! Surely, it would be worth it, to be free from fear...

Where was that bus? Peter was cold as well as wet, and, for the first time in several weeks, he felt ravenously hungry. He peered into the darkness. Did those headlights in the distance belong to an approaching bus or a lorry? He couldn't tell. But behind him—what was that?! He heard a sudden snap of twigs and rustle of leaves in the hedge beside the shelter.

Something—or someone—was moving in the bushes!!

Peter's heart lurched and thudded. Oh no! Was it? It couldn't be! Had the bullies come back to attack him?!

While Peter was waiting, wet and miserable, at the bus stop, Gloria and Jessamy were sitting together in a warm and cosy front room.

"Milk or juice?" called Gloria's mom. She appeared, tall and welcoming, in the doorway. "And would either of you like a sandwich?"

She turned to Ruby, who was putting her coat on in the kitchen. "And what about you? If you're going to the movies tonight, will you want to eat here first?"

"No thanks, Mom," said Ruby. "I'm going to that new pizza place with Jason and Sophie from the salon."

She looked at the clock on the kitchen wall. "Is that the time?! I'd better get going! See you later!"

Jessamy had gone to Gloria's house so that the two of them could practice their dance together—when the Fox chases the Duck round and round the pond, and finally catches her! They had found the music on the Internet and downloaded it onto Jessamy's tablet. Already, Miss Francisco had given all the dancers sheets of paper with all their steps written down, one after the other, in sequence.

Some senior students at the ballet school were taking classes in notation—a clever code used by dancers all round the world to record the sequence of steps in everything from a single dance to a complete ballet performance. But Gloria and Jessamy were too young for that. So they relied on Miss Francisco's notes, and their own ballet memories.

"How you remember it all, I do not know!" exclaimed Gloria's mom. "And it must be difficult having to learn all those French names for the steps that you're doing."

"Not really, Mom," said Gloria. "It sort of sinks into your brain over the years. From almost the very first classes, teachers use French names for the steps they teach us. I've been learning ballet for—what?—four, five years now. I don't even have to think about the names; they're just second nature."

"You should hear Miss Francisco talk about them, though!" giggled Jessamy. She pulled a serious face and stood very straight, in just the same way as their teacher when she took her place in front of the whole ballet class.

"Are you LISTENING, Class 3?" she began, in a slow, serious voice. "We call it TRADITION." Jessamy was an excellent mimic, and always got good marks for any mime she did in her exam dances. "FRENCH is the language of DANCE. It is used WORLDWIDE. That's why dancers from MANY LANDS can learn to perform TOGETHER; they all use the SAME words for the SAME steps!"

Gloria's mom laughed out loud. "Jessamy, that's very naughty!" she said. "I hope Miss Francisco doesn't catch you pretending to be her! Now, does anyone want another drink or anything else to eat?"

"Now, Jess," said Gloria. "I'm the Duck and I'm swimming round in the pond…"

"Here's the music!" Jessamy found it on her tablet:

"*Waaaaaaah, mwa, mwa, mwaaaaah-wha, wah-waaaah,*" went the clarinet.

"Then I get out of the pond—hop, skip, and

jump!—and you try to catch me..."

Jessamy suddenly switched characters to act like a cat out hunting: tense, alert and prowling around.

"I'm so silly," Gloria continued—"NOT in real life, Jess! Stop laughing!—in the ballet story! There, I'm so happy in the sunshine that I simply don't see you."

"Meow! Meow!" said Jessamy, still laughing.

"Right," Jessamy continued, "Here I go! I creep round the pond..." I *galop* sideways, very slowly—with several *petits jetés...* Then you get out of the pond and I chase you."

"Hang on a minute! It says *"changements [shifting my weight from one foot to another]"* on my sheet here. How are we going to manage that?"

"Like this, I think!" Gloria walked across the room, and tried a few careful steps.

"See! I think that works." She smiled. "Let's try it again."

Galop

Back at the bus stop, Peter was still alone in the shelter. Where was everyone this evening? Perhaps the rain was keeping them indoors. He was busy telling himself very firmly to be brave. "I must have imagined that noise," he muttered. "Or it must have been the wind. There's no one there."

But then the bushes rustled again. As well as hearing them, this time Peter saw some branches move. That wasn't the wind. There really was something there, quite close, and hidden in the darkness.

Peter froze with terror.

Chapter 6

Big Bad Wolf

There was a street lamp close to the bus stop. It cast a pool of eerie orange light on the shelter and the wet, uneven pavement nearby. But beyond that, everything looked extra dark. Too scared to move from the shelter, Peter peered out into the gloom, trying to see just what terrible thing was lurking in the bushes.

If the bullies were hiding there, why hadn't they leapt out to attack him by now? Usually, they didn't wait around, or else—like the time when they painted his soccer boots—they played their mean tricks in secret.

If the rustling was a ghost—and it couldn't

be a ghost; Peter didn't believe in them—why would it haunt this bus stop? It was one of the least spooky places in the universe.

So what was there? What was it doing? And what was it going to do next?

Whatever it was, it was definitely still there. The bushes creaked and trembled again. Bravely—perhaps foolishly—Peter took a step toward the hedge.

There! He could see something now. A bright brown eye, watching—watching HIM—with a very wary expression.

Peter stepped back quickly into the shelter.

There was more rustling and snapping of twigs as the first brown eye was joined by a second one. They stared—or was that glared?—straight at Peter.

"Errrm! Hrrumph!" Peter cleared his throat. He *had* to know what was going on. "It's Peter," he said. "I'm here! Who are you? Who's there?"

He hoped his voice sounded less nervous

than he felt. "Why are you looking at me? What are you doing there?!"

Then, all of a sudden, the bushes growled. "Grrrrrrrr! Grrrrrrrr!"

Darcey, who loved animals, could have told him that it was a warning growl—a sign of fear—not a fierce, attacking one. But Peter didn't know that.

Slowly, the leaves parted and a damp black nose appeared below the bright brown eyes.

"Heeeelllp!" Peter cried out in astonishment as what seemed to be a huge wolf's head—huge fangs, long muzzle, pointed ears—peered out of the bushes.

There was more rustling, and the head was joined by sturdy shoulders, a solid body, long legs, big, heavy paws (what long sharp claws!) and a wonderful bushy tail.

It was a magnificent creature. Its thick, fluffy coat was brindled gray and brown; a ruff of longer hair covered its throat and shoulders making it look even bigger. Sharp pointed teeth gleamed yellowish in the street light. As it panted, mouth half-open, it sent little clouds of steam into the cold evening air. It growled again, and wagged its tail.

Was it really a wolf, or just the largest German Shepherd dog that Peter had ever seen?

"Sit!" he said, nervously. But nothing happened. Was it a wolf, after all?!

"Sit!" he said, this time more firmly, and the great beast squatted down on its haunches.

Peter gave a sigh of relief. But what now? What should he do?

The Wolf Dog was still sitting close to Peter, staring up into his face. What was it trying to tell him? What did it want? It panted again. Puff! Puff! Puff! And, rather cautiously, wagged its tail a little bit more.

Peter looked around for someone to help him, but the street seemed deserted. Perhaps he should leave it in the shelter and walk to the next bus stop? That might be worth a try.

"Stay!" he said to Wolf Dog, and began to walk away. He'd only moved a few paces when Wolf Dog got to its feet, shook itself all over, and trotted after him.

"No!" said Peter. "Why are you following me?!"

Together, they returned to the bus stop.

Peter was really worried now. But he must try not to panic. "Good boy!" he said. "Good boy!"

Wolf Dog gazed up at him, watching his every move. It still seemed quite friendly. But Peter was not used to dogs, so how could he be sure? He felt trapped—he *was* trapped—by this big and beautiful beast.

Very, very carefully, Peter reached into his jacket pocket, pulled out his phone and called his mom.

"Peter! Where are you?! I was getting worried! Are you OK? Did you miss the bus...?"

At the other end of the phone, Peter's mom sounded anxious and flustered. In the background, Peter could hear his baby brother George wailing loudly. "Where are you?" she asked. "Are you still at ballet?"

"I'm at the bus stop, Mom," said Peter. "But I can't come home. There's a *wolf* here with me!"

"Peter!" said his mother, crossly. "Don't be silly! Now tell me properly. What's going on?"

"I'm telling the truth, Mom!" said Peter. He was also pretty upset by now. "It looks like a wolf, but it might just be a big dog. It came out of the bushes at the bus stop. Now it won't leave me alone. I've tried walking away but it just follows. If I stand still, it sits down very close and stares at me. It's scary, Mom! What shall I do?" Peter's voice wavered.

His mother's voice sounded suddenly very loud. "DON'T TOUCH IT, PETER!" she said.

"Do you understand? And don't make any sudden movements or loud noises. You don't want to startle it. Just stay where you are and keep calm. Jane's out and your dad's at work, so I'm here alone. But I'll put George in his carry cot and call a taxi straight away. Just stay there—AND DON'T TOUCH THE DOG—and I'll be with you as soon as I can! Okay?"

"Yes, Mom," said Peter. The phone line went dead, and he and Wolf Dog were alone together once again.

Just a few minutes later, car headlights flickered through the rain, and a taxi drew up beside the kerb. Inside the shelter, Wolf Dog's ears pricked up, warily. It got to its feet, took a few cautious steps, and peered toward the car.

As the taxi came to a halt, Peter's mom finished speaking to the driver. "Please can you wait here and look after the baby for just a few minutes until my husband arrives?"

"No problem," said the driver, and switched off the engine.

Slowly, gently, so as not to frighten Wolf Dog, Peter's mom got out of the taxi. She saw Peter and Wolf Dog huddled together at the far end of the bus shelter. The big creature looked calm enough, and quite friendly, as Peter had said. But you never could be sure with strange animals. And this was one of the biggest dogs she had ever seen…

Hands carefully by her side, taking slow, cautious steps, she walked toward them.

"There's a good dog,' she said, very quietly. "We're friends. We're not going to hurt you…'

She stood still for a bit, so the dog could catch the smell of her, and get used to her presence.

Wolf Dog turned toward her—ears alert, sniffing gently. It got up and took a few rather doubtful steps toward her. "That's right,' said

Peter's mom, encouragingly. "Come here!"

Wolf Dog was much closer now, sniffing her shoes and her jeans. A damp patch on one knee seemed particularly interesting. "Peter!" said his mom, in an urgent whisper. "Get out of the shelter! Now! Walk away very slowly and climb into the taxi. Then stay there!"

Wolf Dog licked the knee of her jeans with a rough pink tongue and then opened its mouth, displaying its terrifying teeth. But this was a yawn, not a snarl. Suddenly, it wagged its tail, and snuffled its nose into Peter's mom's pockets. Ah yes—there were a couple of the hard teething biscuits that she'd been giving to baby George. She offered one to Wolf Dog. It sniffed again, took it eagerly, then flopped down on her feet to crunch it up.

"What's going on?" Peter's dad climbed out of his car and walked slowly into the shelter.

Wolf Dog turned its head and looked up, suddenly nervous. Hurriedly, Peter's mom gave it the second biscuit.

"Shh!" she whispered to Peter's dad. "The kids are safe in the taxi. Don't startle the dog. I've just about got it settled."

Peter's dad went back to his car and fetched a long, strong tow-rope. While Peter's mom talked soothingly to Wolf Dog, he threaded the rope though its collar and fastened it with a double knot. Then he tied the other end of the rope to the bus shelter.

Thankfully, Wolf Dog didn't seem to mind. Instead, he sniffed Peter's dad's pockets for food, in a hopeful way.

"Sorry, mate! You're out of luck!" said Peter's dad. "These are my best work pants. No biscuits there!"

"Look!" he went on, as he parted Wolf Dog's

thick coat to get at its leather collar. There's a metal tag here, with a phone number. I'll read it out to you—can you write it down?"

Peter's mom fumbled in her pockets again and found a crayon and a crumpled scrap of paper. "Go ahead," she said. Then her voice changed. "Peter! What are you doing here? I told you to stay in the taxi!" she cried in alarm.

"It's OK, Mom," said Peter. "I saw that Dad had tied Wolf Dog to the shelter, so I reckoned it was safe to come out."

"Just don't get too close," warned his dad. "Strange dogs can't be trusted."

Wolf Dog yawned, and sat down. Peter's mom went to get baby George from the taxi, and pay the driver. He revved the car's engine, and, muttering to himself about "dangerous wild beasts," drove off into the night.

Hand in hand, Peter, his mom and his dad stood at a safe distance from Wolf Dog and breathed deep sighs of relief. From the end of the tow-rope, Wolf Dog gazed back at them. It wagged its tail, just once or twice, and whimpered softly.

"Poor thing!" said Peter's mom. "It's lonely and frightened. You know, I think that it's really pleased that we've found it. Now, let's call that number!"

Chapter 7
Preparations

illow had finished her dinner, had a shower and changed into her PJs. She had brushed her teeth and twisted her long hair into a loose plait (it got badly tangled overnight, otherwise). Now she walked slowly from the bathroom to her bedroom. Her mom was right; she was tired. Sleepily, she yawned and rubbed her eyes.

She found her mom in her bedroom, sitting on the end of the bed. In one hand, she held a bag of dirty ballet clothes, ready to put in the washing machine. In the other, she held a printed letter.

Willow's mom looked up from the page. "Oh dear!" she sighed. "I thought I'd found out all I needed to know when I checked the noticeboards at the Ballet School. But now there's this letter about your end of semester show. The Ballet School secretary gave us all a copy while we were waiting for your class to finish. I put it in your ballet bag; I've only just remembered it!

"It's very helpful, really—there's a checklist of all you need to bring for the dress rehearsal and on the day of the performance. But there's such a lot you need! And look—it also gives dates and times of several extra rehearsals. There's one next Tuesday after school, for fitting costumes... I didn't know about that. Did you?"

Her voice trailed off, and she smiled at Willow reassuringly. "Oh, don't worry, love! We'll manage! But the next few weeks will be extra busy for me. I'll be starting to work long training shifts at the big city hospital. Your dad will just have to forget about his bikes for a few days, and start to learn a bit more about ballet!"

She laughed. "Who knows, he may even take it up! I've heard it's very good for building strong leg muscles, and that's exactly what cyclists need... Anyway, it's certainly true what they say: 'A ballet child means a ballet family!'"

Willow giggled at the thought of her tall, tough and very clumsy dad joining in the ballet class. "Let's see, Mom!" she said, and peered over her mother's shoulder at the list.

- *Dressing gown*
- *Slippers or indoor shoes*
- *Soap and towel or cleanser to remove makeup*

- *Hairbrush*
- *Hair clips, gel, hairnet (as required)*
- *Bottle of water*

- *Light snack (no potato chips, no nuts)*
- *Piece of fruit*
- *Soft toy if wanted (one only)*

- *Book or electronic reader*
- *Notebook and pencil (no pens or felt tips)*
- *Tablet or similar (headphones essential)*

- **NO CELL PHONES!**

"That's quite some list!" said Willow, laughing.

"And look at this here!" Willow's mom read some more of the letter out loud: "'All students playing Birds will need red ballet shoes.' Not *another* pair! Don't they know how much they cost!?... And there are all those ribbons to sew on...

"Oh well. If the red shoes don't get much wear before you grow out of them, I expect another child will be able to use them. We can pass them on. And if I can't take you to the ballet store to get them properly fitted, then perhaps you can go with Jessamy and her mom?

Jessamy has a part, doesn't she? Ah yes. See! It says here: 'Cat: black shoes'—Jessamy will need to get those; they're normally only for boys. And what's this?" Willow's mom looked puzzled. "'Cat: black gloves'. What's that for?"

"Paws, Mom," said Willow.

Willow's mom laughed. "Of course," she said.

"I'm glad that one of us is on the ball." She gave Willow a big hug. "My smart, ballet-mad daughter. Now, into bed with you!"

Across the other side of the city, Darcey was also getting ready for bed. But, unlike Willow, her mind was not on her dancing. She had meant what she said as she'd left the ballet school. She would learn her steps, so as not to spoil the dance for her friends. In fact, she'd practiced them again, soon after she got home, hoping to fix them firmly in her memory.

"Do you know, Class," Miss Francisco had said one day, "that our muscles have memories? They are linked very closely to the memory center in our brain. That's why we practice ballet movements over and over again. The practice makes our steps neat and precise, of course, and that's extremely important.

Sometimes even an *inch* out of place can be crucial. Just think about members of the corps de ballet. They often have to keep perfectly in step with dancers on either side. Their feet make amazing patterns as they dance—the smallest mistake can ruin the effect.

"But that's not all. By practicing and repeating movements over and over again, our muscles remember them and we can perform them almost without thinking. Professional dancers do classes every day to keep their bodies strong and flexible, but also to make sure that they don't forget their steps—the basic building blocks of every dance."

Darcey had pinned Miss Francisco's notes showing the full sequence of her dance to the wall above her bed. She looked at them the moment she woke up, and as she fell asleep. She had briefly thought about putting them under her pillow every night so that she could sleep on top of them. Some ballet school students were convinced that this helped them to learn better. But privately Darcey thought that was stupid.

"Do they really believe," she scoffed (silently), "that the ink and the instructions somehow come off the page and sink into their brain!?" Clearly, that was impossible. It was so unscientific!!

Darcey wanted to be a scientist—a scientist who studied animals. Right now, she did her best to prepare for her scientific future by working hard in math and science, and by observing the family pets.

Tonight, she'd watched closely as her pet mice tiptoed delicately along the bars of the climbing frame in their cage, using their tails to help them balance.

What neat, precise footwork! she had thought, admiringly. Better than most ballerinas. But if you looked closely, you could see that their feet were completely different from human feet; they used their claws to hold on tight. Having four feet obviously gave them much better balance than two!

Later, as she'd stroked the soft, silky fur of Boris, their scruffy old cat, she'd felt the big strong muscles of his back legs, relaxed now as he purred contentedly, but still tough and springy under his saggy, baggy skin.

Her father, who was already a scientist working for a big corporation, noticed what Darcey was doing. "That's what gives Boris the power to leap so far and so fast," he said. "Though his best jumping days are over. Compare the size of his back legs—relative to the rest of his body—to the legs and bodies of humans. Old Boris here can leap several times his own height. Just imagine what it would be like if all you ballet dancers had leg muscles as big as cats, and could leap like them too!"

Darcey went to bed smiling, her mind full of pictures of ballet stars with huge muscles

leaping and bounding high off the stage
and soaring out over the orchestra and the
audience. She fell fast asleep before they
landed. Which was probably a good thing.

Back home after the movie, Ruby sat at her
mom's kitchen table and made a long To Do
list. Next week was going to be very busy for
everyone at Rosewood Ballet School.

Chapter 8
Superstars

eanwhile, back at the bus shelter, Peter and his dad stood impatiently waiting as Peter's mom talked to an unknown person on her phone. She had rung the number on Wolf Dog's metal tag. Almost straight away, a male voice had answered.

"We think we have your dog!" Mom had said. "Yes! A giant German Shepherd. We rang the number on its collar. Oh yes, it's alive. And well. But rather frightened and lonely."

Father and son looked at one another, and sighed. Once mom got going, she loved to chat. From experience they knew this might take some time.

From the car, they heard the unhappy wails of poor, teething, baby George.

"I'll go and see if I can calm him," said Peter's dad. "You can stay here if you like—but don't go anywhere near that dog!"

Peter moved closer to his mom, trying to hear what she was saying. Wolf Dog seemed to be listening, too.

"Hello? Hello?" Peter's mom pressed the phone close to her ear as two buses—now they were here!—thundered past.

Peter heard a deep voice at the other end of the phone, but he could not make out what the unknown man was saying.

"Oh, yes. Yes." His mom chattered on. "The dog's fine. It's rather dirty and very hungry, but there's no sign of any injury. We found it—well, my son found it—in the bushes next to the big parking lot, down by the train station. It just appeared. I've no idea where from…"

She turned to Peter. "Do you know?"

Peter shook his head. "I didn't see it when I went into the ballet school, but it might have been hiding."

His mom was speaking into her phone again. "It's been missing for how long?! What? Kidnapped?! A ransom note?! Did you tell the police? Mmm … yes… yes… Well… I suppose they are very busy.

"So when you wouldn't pay the ransom, they let it go? No? Mmmm… mmmmm… mmmm… More likely it escaped, you think? Well, it is very big and it must be really strong… Oh, yes. Very gentle, so far…

"No. No. It's not too thin. I expect it's found some scraps to eat. There's so much trash round the back of those cafés by the station. But I wonder where it's been hiding during the day?

"You'll come to get it? Right now? That's great! You know where we are? At the bus

stop by the Rosewood Ballet School. Mmmm…
Across the parking lot. That's right. Turn left
after the lights. The dog's quite safe. Don't
worry. We'll look after it until you get here. By-
ee! See you soon!"

By now, it was completely dark. Wolf Dog's
eyes shone with a reddish glow as they reflected
lights from the passing traffic, but Peter was
too tired to notice. His mom was speaking,
again. "I think Dad should take you and George
back home, and put you both to bed. You're
exhausted. I can walk home by myself, once I've
handed Wolf Dog here over to its owner."

Peter's dad came back from the car. "What?"
he said. "May, don't be silly. You can't wait
here in the dark for a strange man, all alone!
And what if that dog turns vicious, and attacks
you?"

Peter's mom looked very cross. "This is the 21st century! I don't need a man to protect me!"

"Be reasonable, Maisie," said Peter's dad. "That dog's owner could be anyone! I'm staying, anyway."

"He sounded fine on the phone," said Peter's mom. "Very polite, in fact. And ever so grateful! He had a foreign accent—German, I think, or something like that..."

While his parents argued, Peter leaned against the back of the bus shelter and let his weary mind drift off into a dream. First he was hugging Wolf Dog. Its coat was warm and comforting, like a huge furry blanket. Its steady breathing, in and out, in and out, soothed him like a wordless lullaby. But then the dream got darker. The bullies were coming to get him! They were getting closer, closer... But Wolf Dog raced toward them, fangs bared, barking loudly, and chased them away.

Peter was woken by the sound of car doors slamming, followed by loud, cheerful voices and the sound of real-life barking: Woof, Woof, WOOF! He opened his eyes to see two good-looking, athletic young men shaking his parents by the hand—and then kneeling on the ground to hug Wolf Dog. They unknotted the rope that tied him to the shelter and set him free. Wolf Dog was frantic with excitement—barking, wagging his tail, licking the men's faces and bouncing around.

"I'm Matthias,' said the young man with the German accent, "Wolfie here belongs to me." He smiled at Peter's mother. "Thank you! Thank you for finding him. It is so good to have him back…"

Wolf Dog sprang up suddenly and licked

Matthias's face yet again; even the strong young man staggered a bit. Then it slunk a few steps away and sat down—looking rather ashamed of itself—after Matthias said something short and sharp in German.

"He's a great dog," Matthias continued. "So big, but so gentle—except when he thinks he's in danger. Or, of course, if anyone attacks me. He's far too excited right now, but I think that is understandable. I was devastated when he was snatched from his kennel last week. Somehow, thieves cut through the high fence that runs around my garden. That set off the burglar alarms, so they didn't get inside my house. But they managed to grab poor old Wolfie as they ran away. Then they sent a ransom demand by text to my manager.

I don't know how long they had him. Possibly he jumped out the first time they opened the doors of their van. He is not easy to hold! Anyway, he is back now. And that is all that matters."

A dark haired, dark skinned young man stepped forward. "This is my friend, Romeo," Matthias said.

"Pleased to meet you," smiled Romeo. He had a soft, musical accent. Was he Portuguese? Or perhaps Brazilian? Romeo spoke again. "We are having dinner with some of the team—just quietly, at Matthias's home, because we have a big game on Sunday. Then the phone rings. It is you, with news of Wolfie. That is wonderful!

Except when he scores a goal, I don't think I ever see Matthias so excited. So we really, really, thank you. Now my friend will play very well on Sunday!"

While the two men were talking, Peter caught sight of their car. Bright red, streamlined, sleek and shiny, very powerful, super fast... Wow! It was fantastic! Then he overheard the words "team" and "goal."

Suddenly, in astonishment, Peter realized

who the young men were. He recognized their faces. He'd seen them before, not in real life—but on TV. They were Matthias Steller and Romeo de Branco, the latest celebrity signings to the city's soccer team. Now here they were, chatting away quite happily to his mom and dad, as if they were old friends.

"Oh, don't thank me!" said Peter's mom. "Peter was the one who found Wolfie. He was on his way home from ballet class…"

Peter groaned. Why oh why did his mom have to mention ballet in front of two famous soccer players?! He was so ashamed. If only the ground would open up beneath his feet and swallow him! He felt sure that these sports stars would think that ballet was strange and silly—and that he was silly, too.

Peter's mother talked on. "He's quite good at it, really. The funny thing is, he's got a big part in the ballet school end of semester show." She waved her arm vaguely across the parking lot toward the ballet school building. "And guess what? He's playing a wolf!"

"Haha!" laughed Romeo, politely. "But ballet, you say? That is interesting!" He turned to talk to Peter. "We do ballet exercises twice every week when we train. Our coach is a big ballet fan. He says that ballet gives us speed, strength, control AND balance! That can't be bad!

"It's hard work, though." Romeo looked thoughtful. "All that footwork isn't as easy as it looks." Laughing, he turned out his toes in a wildly exaggerated fifth position, and bent his knees in a series of pretend *pliés*. "But it sure helps our game. So well done! Keep on dancing, young Peter!"

He smiled again. "I know one world-class player trained for years as a dancer before he turned to soccer. I'm sure there will be others…"

Romeo turned to call his friend. "Hey! Matthias, come here! You need to meet this young man. He's the one who found your

Wolfie!"

Matthias stopped stroking Wolf Dog, and came across to where Peter was standing. "I am so grateful," he said, looking suddenly, surprisingly, serious. "The dog means a lot to me. I must find a way to say a proper 'thank you'. I will save your mother's number on my phone, and I will get in touch with her soon. That is a promise!"

"But now," Peter's mom interrupted. "We must go home! It's way past Peter's bedtime. It was very nice to meet you both," she shook their hands again. "I'm so pleased you've got your dog back!"

The soccer players strolled back to their car, Wolf Dog trotting happily behind them. "Goodbye! Thank you!"

As the red car sped away, Peter thought he heard a parting "Woof Woof" above the roar of its engine.

Chapter 9
On The Team

It was Monday; school day. After spending a quiet weekend at home, Peter was feeling decidedly nervous. Deliberately, defiantly, he had kicked a soccer ball around the back yard, but had *not* done any ballet practice.

The excitement of finding Wolf Dog and meeting the soccer stars had faded all too quickly. Now he felt as dull and gray as the winter weather outside. His mom and dad hadn't noticed—or, more probably, they had, and just thought he was still tired after the late night on Friday. But for Peter, life was back to normal again, and full of his old worries.

He knew he'd given up ballet, but the bullies didn't. So what awful things might they be planning to do to him today on the way back home from school? Just the feeling of fear was enough to make him groan.

Peter flopped down at the breakfast table. Helpfully, his mom tipped some breakfast cereal into a bowl, and poured milk over.

"Do you want toast, as well?" she asked. "But don't be too long. Look at the time! We're late! You've got to be ready to leave in less than ten minutes."

"No thanks, Mom," Peter said. He pushed his cereal around the bowl with his spoon. He wasn't hungry. All he could think of was the trouble that—almost certainly—lay in wait for him.

Should he tell the bullies he'd dropped out of ballet? Would that be sensible? Probably not; they'd know they'd won. And how should he do it, anyway? He could hardly stand up in the middle of the classroom and make an announcement. He'd look a right idiot, and the bullies probably wouldn't believe him. Peter didn't know what to do.

The first few classes weren't too bad. First math, then English. Then science, where they were finding out about levers. If he'd been feeling better, Peter might have realized that understanding how levers worked could have helped him with some of his dance moves. But today, he was trying to keep the ballet part of his brain firmly shut away.

Thankfully, his friends Zac and Wiktor were sitting beside him all morning. Wiktor had exciting news. He and his family were going back to Poland, for a whole fortnight, over Christmas.

"Dad booked the tickets at the weekend,"

Viktor said. "We leave at the start of the school holidays. I can't wait to see my Dziadzio and Babunia again. And I've got lots of cousins who I really want to meet up with. I haven't seen them for at least two years. I wonder if I'll recognize them! Or if they'll recognize me! They live close to the Tatry Wysokie mountains. If the weather's good, my uncle says he'll take me ice-climbing with them. I really want to learn!

There's a climbing wall in this city," he pulled a face. "But it's not like the real mountains, and the classes are SOOO expensive."

The end of semester was when he should have been dancing in Peter and the Wolf, thought Peter. He wished he could go far away, like Wiktor. Then the bullies wouldn't be able to get him...

The bell rang for the end of class, and the boys trooped out into the playground. Nearly lunchtime. Would Peter be able to get to the boys' bathroom (another place where the bullies lurked) and back to the school hall in safety? He made a quick dash, and, rather breathless, returned to join Zac and Wiktor in the lunch line.

Mr Jones appeared from the far end of the corridor. "Ah, Peter! Good!" he said. "I've been looking for you! I want to see some of our soccer players before afternoon classes. Come to the changing room in about 20 minutes." He looked at his watch. "I'll be waiting there. Now—has anybody seen JJ?"

Peter ate a hasty lunch. If anyone had asked him, he couldn't have said what the food was. His thoughts were all over the place. Zac and Wiktor were talking together...

"Hey, Pete," said Zac. "Watch out! You've just put your sleeve in the tomato sauce!"

Peter twisted his sleeve round; a sinister looking stain was spreading outward from his elbow. Peter shuddered. It looked just like blood. That was his biggest fear; that one of the bullies would have a knife, and, one day, would stab him...

"Thanks, Zac," he said, mopping the stain. Zac got up, and began to walk toward the serving hatch where the lunch-helpers dished out food.

"Coming to get dessert?" he asked. Peter shook his head. "No thanks," he said. "Anyway, it's almost time to go and see Mr Jones."

Zac shrugged. "Okay! See you later," he said. He turned back to speak to Wiktor. "Pete's in a strange mood today. I wonder if something's the matter?"

As Peter walked across the drafty playground toward the playing fields and changing rooms, he wondered why Mr Jones wanted to see him. Mondays weren't the usual day for soccer

training; anyway, that was always later in
the afternoon, after school. Peter enjoyed
the training sessions. Mr Jones was a burly,
cheerful man with a loud voice and a quick (but
thankfully short-lived) temper, who took a real
interest in his students. He let anyone who
was keen come along to his Tuesday training
sessions. (The second one, on Wednesdays, was
for team members only.) It didn't matter how
good or bad they were. So long as they tried,
and worked hard, and were willing to learn, he
was happy to teach them new skills.

Peter opened the changing room door, and
stepped slowly inside. The place was empty!
Where were the other soccer players? He was
puzzled.

Mr Jones's voice rang out across the
changing room from his desk in the far corner.
It sounded strange, almost like an echo, as it
bounced off the shiny painted walls and rows
of metal coat hooks, benches and lockers. "Ah!

Peter!" he boomed. "Thank you for coming to see me. The other boys will be here in just a few minutes." He looked at his watch again. "But before they arrive, I'd like to have a word with you, in private.

"Your mom phoned me this morning. She'd just heard from Miss Francisco at the Ballet School about what happened on Friday evening. She couldn't believe that you wanted to give up ballet, and wondered if I knew why. I don't know, of course, but perhaps I can make a guess. Is it anything to do with the bullies?"

Peter couldn't speak, but he nodded, miserably.

Mr Jones went on, "I haven't told your mom about them,' he said. "Though I will do if you'd like me to. Perhaps that would be helpful?"

Peter shook his head.

"Okay. That's fine," said Mr Jones. "You know our policy. The school will keep what you say completely confidential—unless breaking the law is involved, or we judge that you're in danger.

"Over the weekend, I've been thinking about those bullies, and how we can stop them. I've asked the teachers and their assistants to be on the lookout, so we can step in and deal with the offenders. We're planning an assembly about bullying next week, and we've asked someone from the community police to come and give a talk.

"I've also heard of a traveling theater team that puts on plays about bullying then runs workshops for students afterward. They're very popular, so they're quite booked up. But don't worry—we'll get them here somehow!

"However, if the bullies attack you outside school, then that's rather more difficult for us teachers to tackle. We have no legal powers outside the school gates."

Mr Jones looked straight at Peter. "I really think that you should tell your parents about what's been happening; maybe one of them, or another adult, could collect you by car for a while? Or could you go home by a different route? Or walk part of the way with friends…?

"We need to make it difficult for the bullies to know where you're going to be. That way, they won't be lying in wait. Eventually, if they can't find you, they'll get bored and lose interest."

Peter didn't know what to say.

Mr Jones continued. "More than all that, I've had another idea. We can get going with it right now…"

The changing room door opened with a clumsy bang. JJ and Arif walked in, closely followed by the rest of the soccer team, including some of the bullies.

"Right on time! Over here, lads!" boomed Mr Jones. "Come and meet our newest team member."

Peter gasped.

"Peter will be a very valuable new player,"

said Mr Jones. "He's fast, he's light on his feet, and he's very accurate. I'm sure you've seen him score some fantastic goals in training sessions, so it's high time he joined us. Now he'll be scoring goals for our team, and—I hope—helping us win lots of matches."

"He'll come to the next team-only training session, on Wednesday afternoon. You must help him all you can."

Arif and JJ grinned at Peter from the far side of the room. "Wheee-ee!" whistled JJ. "Cool!" shouted Arif.

Mr Jones's voice changed.

"I called you all here for another reason, as well. Today, the school is starting a new campaign, and I expect all team members—and that means every single one of you,"—Mr Jones thumped the desk with his fist, to emphasise the words—"to play a leading part in it. The rest of the school looks up to you. So you must all set a good example. The campaign is very important—just as important as soccer."

Some of the boys laughed, disbelievingly. They were the keenest members of the team. They lived for the game. Could anything be more important? Mr Jones glared at them, fiercely. "Oh yes it is. It's very, very important. And I mean what I say." Mr Jones's voice was stern. "Everyone must join in. Or else they're out of the team. Our campaign is against cruel, stupid, unsportsmanlike behavior. It's called Kick Bullying Out Of School."

Chapter 10

...And in the News

Once Mr Jones had finished speaking, and sent the team—including Peter!—back for afternoon classes, Peter rushed to find Zac and Wiktor and tell them his news. They were standing outside the art room, waiting for the teacher to arrive.

"Wooo-ee!" said Zac, leaping up for a high-five. Wiktor joined in. "Hey! I'm so pleased for you, Peter my friend. Peter my friend and top soccer player!"

Peter laughed. A proper, happy laugh. For what seemed the first time in years.

The rest of the afternoon passed in a blur.

Peter tried hard to concentrate on the design he was making on one of the art room computers, but he found it very difficult. Deep inside him, a little voice seemed to be singing, "I'm in the team! I'm in the team!" It felt *really* good.

Finally it was time to go home. He didn't see any sign of the bullies, but, just for now, he felt strong enough to face anything. He'd always been a fast runner. This afternoon, his feet practically flew along the road.

It wasn't long before he reached home. He slammed the back door behind him in his haste to rush into the kitchen. There he found his mom, looking really worried.

"Is George OK?" he asked in a sudden panic. "And Jane? And Dad?"

"Oh, Peter," said his mom. "They're all fine! It's *you* I'm worried about. I had a phone call this morning from Miss Francisco at the ballet school. She says you were really unhappy during the class on Friday. And—I can hardly believe I'm saying this—she says that you shouted at her. She also says—is this really true?—that you want to give up ballet."

"Yes, it's all true, Mom," said Peter, impatiently. "But—listen to this! Today I got picked for the school soccer team! A full member, not just a reserve!"

Peter's mom did a bit of very, very quick thinking.

"Well, that's wonderful!" she said. "That's brilliant news! Come here! I'm so proud of you, Peter! And so will your dad be, once he gets home and hears all about it." And she gave him a big, big hug.

Later that afternoon, Peter was sitting on the sofa, with his reading book on his knees. He had to finish it by the following week, and write a report on it to present to the rest of his class. He was rather more full of celebration ice cream than was ideal for a sportsman in training. But, as his mom had said, it was not every day that you got selected for the school team. And Peter had eaten very little breakfast and almost no lunch.

"Just this once, it will do no harm," said his mom. "Tomorrow, I'll have another word with Mr Jones and see what he recommends. We need to feed you very healthily now you're a team member."

Peter was naturally slight and skinny; ballet had made him strong. To do his best on the soccer field, he wanted to stay that way. He knew his mom would help him.

Baby George sat propped up on the sofa, close beside Peter. "Gah, gah, gah!" he said, smiling, seeming to connect with Peter's happy mood. Their mom was pottering about between the kitchen and the sitting room. "Keep an eye on George, please!" she called to Peter. I just need to get dinner going."

In the corner of the kitchen, a small television set flickered black and white then brightly-colored. A tinny signature tune blared out around the room. Deep in his reading book, and keeping a firm hold on George with one hand, Peter hardly noticed it.

Suddenly, his mom's excited voice made him look up. "Peter! Quick! Quick! Come and see this..." She scooped baby George up in her arms, and they all hurried into the kitchen.

It was the local TV news. Peter's mom pointed to the screen. It showed soccer players Matthias and Romeo, and Wolf Dog, too, outside the city team headquarters. Matthias was talking to the TV interviewer. "Yes, I've had Wolfie for three years. He's a wonderful friend."

Wolfie's big wet nose filled the TV screen. "Ooops!" said the TV interviewer. "Don't eat the camera!"

Matthias continued. "The boy who found him? Well, I met him on Friday and was able to say 'thank you' in person. I'm so pleased that he brought Wolfie back to me. He's my lucky mascot." He laughed. "You know, I think I play much better when Wolfie's in the directors' box, close to the pitch."

"What about the boy? That's not for me to say. You must ask his parents. All that I will share is that his name was Peter and he had been to ballet classes. He was waiting at the bus stop…" The screen showed a still photo of Rosewood Ballet School and the parking lot looking rather drab in the rain. "He was very helpful and sensible. I owe him a lot!"

Romeo stood behind Matthias, smiling broadly. The interviewer turned to question him.

"Yes, I go with Matthias to meet the dog from behind the ballet school," said Romeo. "We are teammates. It is sensible! Who knows who might be phoning? It could be a trap. The caller might want to rob Matthias or kidnap him for a ransom! Or he might threaten to harm the dog. Of course he cannot go to meet the unknown caller alone. No way! There are six or seven of us at dinner. We tell the others where we are going. They promise to follow us, at a distance. They are all ready to call the police if there is any trouble...

"I volunteer to go with Matthias in his car. He drives like a madman to get there! And then we meet—not gangsters, as I half expect—but this very nice family."

"The boy who found Wolfie did good, very good. He is calm and he phones for help. Ahh—I remember—when I am his age I also go to ballet classes. I enjoy them. They make me faster on the field, I think. I still know some steps..."

Laughing, in his sharp tailored suit, Romeo stood on tiptoe, raised his arms above his head and twirled round and round. "See!" he laughed. "Pirouette! Pirouette! I remember!"

"PETER!" shrieked his mom, in amazement. "Did you see that! They're talking about you!"

Pirouette

"And—my goodness!" she went on, "Now I've got a chance to see him properly, that Romeo really is rather handsome! And just look at the dog! Look at his tail—wag, wag, wag! He's clearly very happy. I'm so pleased that he's safely back home."

"There! That's your father's key in the door. He'll be so proud when you tell him about the soccer team!"

Peter's mom didn't want to spoil Peter's evening, so she didn't ask him about ballet. But in spite of Peter's wonderful soccer news, she still felt worried.

Why had Peter burst into tears at the end of the class? Was he over-tired? Was he ill? Why had he shouted at Miss Francisco? (Whatever the reason, she must tell Peter to apologize...) And why did he want to give up ballet all of a sudden? Wouldn't he miss it? Wouldn't he miss all his friends at the ballet school?

Peter's mom sighed. All this would have to wait for now. But she really would have to try to talk to Peter tomorrow.

Peter went off to school the next day with his mind still full of soccer. He was surprised when Zac met him just inside the school gates.

"Why didn't you *tell* us?" said Zac. "Look!" He waved the local newspaper in front of Peter's nose. "Haven't you seen?!"

There was a banner headline: *"Local ballet boy saves soccer star's best friend!"*

There was a low wall close to the school gate. Overwhelmed, Peter suddenly had to sit down.

"It happened on Friday," he said. "It was late. After ballet. There was this huge dog. I thought it was a wolf… Mom phoned the soccer player. I mean, she didn't know it was him. She just phoned the number on the dog's collar, and two soccer players turned up in their amazing car."

"Did you get their autographs?" asked Zac. "Weren't you afraid of the dog?"

Peter shook his head. "No... Not really..." he said.

All day at school, it was the same. People kept asking him about the soccer players and the dog. Peter was a hero—and the bullies left him alone.

Tired out from all the fuss, Peter walked slowly home after school. There was no need to run. He was no longer afraid.

"Peter!" His mom greeted him excitedly as soon as he came into the kitchen. "Matthias has been in touch, and look! He's sent signed photographs of him and Romeo, and tickets for all of us for the big match at the end of the season. Oh—and a photo for you, of Wolfie."

She handed the photos to Peter. He looked at them, then turned them over. The one of Wolfie had writing on the back.

"Thank you!" it said. "To my good friend Peter."

"I've got Matthias's letter here," said Peter's mom. She scrabbled around among papers on the kitchen table and read out loud: *"Very grateful ... helpful young man ... dog-lover... soccer fan...*

"And look at this!' she continued. "There's more:

"If you can tell me the name of the sports teacher at Peter's school, I will offer to talk to his soccer team, and maybe help with a training session one day. And Romeo says that he will talk to students at the ballet class, if they would like to meet him. Please tell us who to contact, and we will be there. Of course, we will mention Peter's name when we write. It will be a good recommendation..."

Peter's mom was positively pink with pleasure and pride. "Oh Peter," she sighed. "How wonderful..."

Of course Peter was pleased, but he was also rather uneasy. What would the ballet school say if Romeo came to talk, and Peter was not there? What did his ballet friends—Willow, Darcey, Gloria, Jessamy and the others—think of his sudden disappearance from class and from rehearsals? And who would take the part of the Wolf in the end of semester performance?

He could only think of one dancer good enough to leap like him, and that was Jessamy. But she already had a part... If she took his, who would take hers? His mind whizzed round and round like one of Darcey's pet mice playing on their exercise wheel.

Right now, he was still too excited about

soccer to answer any of these questions. But, like his mom, he knew they would not go away.

He went to bed early that night. Tomorrow would be Wednesday, and his first time at the training session for team members only. Would he be good enough? He hoped so.

Peter slept well at first, but, some time past midnight, he found himself tossing and turning. He'd been dreaming, but now he was wide awake. He could still remember his dream.

He'd been back at the ballet school, with all his friends. The usual Friday class was just beginning. Willow, Darcey, Jessamy, Gloria, they were all there—and dancing very nicely. But their teacher was Wolf Dog, not Miss Francisco or old Madame Olga. Strangely, Wolf Dog spoke like a human—and wore soccer boots! Even in his dream, Peter knew that this

was utterly ridiculous. But then Wolf Dog—
boots and all—taught him a wonderful new way
to leap. Dreamily, Peter found himself thinking,
"I must use this step in my performance… Let
me remember it: *ballone, ballone, sissonne
fondue….*"

Later that morning, bleary-eyed over
breakfast, Peter remembered his dream again.
A sudden thought struck him. In the dream,
he'd been dancing. Ballet dancing. Better than
ever before.

And he'd really, really enjoyed it.

Chapter 11
Curtain Call

Of course, Peter's ballet friends had seen the TV, and read the newspaper, too.

"That must be *our* Peter!" said Willow, when she heard his name. "How brave he was to stay with that dog and keep it safe until its owner could fetch it! I think I'd have run away."

"Darcey would have known what to do," said Jessamy. "She has a dog of her own and is mad about all kinds of animals."

"And she knows a lot about wildlife," added Gloria. "It's a pity she's not here yet. We could have asked her. But she's late, as usual!"

The three friends were waiting in one of the

smaller practice rooms in the ballet school, along with all the other dancers for the end of semester show.

All except Peter.

It was the day for trying on their costumes. A buzz of excited chatter filled the room. "I can't wait to see our dresses!" said one of the little Flowers. "I hope mine's pink, with glitter!"

"Don't be silly," her friend replied. "Real flowers aren't glittery. It's springtime in the story, so we'll probably be daffodils or something. Or Lilac—like the Lilac Fairy in The Sleeping Beauty. I'd love a lilac costume—purple's my favorite color."

Ruby was already busy at the back of the room, with her arms full of clothes and headdresses. So was Miss Francisco, who was checking items off on a list, and muttering to herself, and frowning.

"Three flower hats..." she muttered. "No, four. But we should have about ten..."

"Bushes for the hunters to carry... Grandfather's stick... Oh, Ruby! Ruby? Did Darren's father say that he would be bringing the tree costume with him?"

"Yes, that's right!" called Ruby. "Well, most of it. It's in several pieces—a big tube for the trunk; I made that from wire and the lightest brown fabric I could find. That's here already. Darren's dad is bringing the leaves and branches. He's cut them out of card and paper."

"Have they been properly fireproofed?" asked Miss Francisco, sharply.

"Yes, yes... don't worry," Ruby replied. "That's all been seen to. A man from the Fire Station came to talk to us. He was really helpful! He told me and the other helpers how to make the costumes safe, and all about fire precautions for the costume store. We've followed his instructions very carefully."

Just then the door flew open and Darcey rushed in, breathless. "Sorry I'm late!" she said.

"We set off with plenty of time today, but the parking lot is completely full! We had to wait until someone drove out before Mom could find a space. Her car's right over on the other side. I ran here as fast as I could. Mom's on her way. She won't be long!"

Miss Francisco looked up from her list.

"All right, Darcey. We believe you. Go and take off your outdoor clothes, put your ballet shoes on, and calm down. And someone— anyone—go and hold that door open for Mr Brown. He needs a hand! Quickly, please!"

Darren's dad walked in slowly, backward, carrying a jumble of cardboard shapes.

"Thank you!" he said to Willow, who had opened the door. "These aren't heavy, but they are pretty awkward!"

He turned to Darren, and said jokingly, "Rather you than me, son! See you later." He went back to his van.

Miss Francisco was giving instructions again.

"Now, boys, when we're ready, Mrs Chang will take you to the next-door practice room, and you can get changed in there. Darcey's mother will collect your costumes from Ruby—you're mostly trees or birds, aren't you?—and bring them in so you can try them on. Then she'll come back and help me.

"Darren, you stay here. You can try on your tree costume over your practice T-shirt and shorts. I know you've got proper brown ones for the performance at home. We don't want to move those branches around any more than necessary. They're great—your father's done a wonderful job!—but they look rather fragile and we don't want to damage them."

The costumes were great, and they nearly all fitted first time round. Willow looked lovely as the Bird. Her "wings"—a sort of cape with flapping sleeves that fastened on each shoulder and wrist—were covered with brightly-colored fake feathers that fluttered with each step she took. She wore scarlet tights and a bright blue leotard, and—Ruby had done a compromise deal with Miss Francisco—a yellow headdress shaped like a bird's beak, and some face-paint. Red ballet shoes would complete the outfit; Jessamy's mom had promised to take Willow with her when they went to the ballet shoe store next week.

Darcey was a slightly untidy flower, with green tights and leotard, a skirt of orange and yellow petals, and a flower-shaped cap on her head.

Gloria made a very elegant Duck, dressed in white and gray, with long yellow leggings and socks, and white ballet shoes.

Jessamy the Cat was clothed from head to toe in a black fleecy costume, with a bib of white fur fabric on the front, and white furry wristbands and ankle-warmers. Lifelike ears, made from black plastic, stuck up from the hood, together with long white whiskers.

"I've planned some fantastic face makeup for you," promised Ruby, "with lots more whiskers. And, talking of facial hair,"—she rummaged in a big box, then turned to Molly, who was already dressed in Grandfather's baggy pants, plaid shirt and braces—"I've got this absolutely wonderful beard for you!"

Molly tried it on. "OOOh, oooh, it tickles!" she shrieked.

Miss Francisco came over. "Molly. Quietly please! Where's your hat? Grandfather should be wearing an old-fashioned cap. Run over to Darcey's mother, please, and ask her whether she's seen it."

Miss Francisco added another note to the growing list on her clipboard.

Away at the back of the room, Ruby carefully

packed Peter's Wolf headdress in tissue paper. She curled the Wolf tail inside the same box. There! Peter's costume was ready! Along with all the students, Ruby did not know what had happened to him, except what she'd heard on the news.

"It's a shame he's not here today. I hope he's OK,' she thought. "He's a good kid. And he'll look great as a Wolf!"

"Now," said Miss Francisco, putting down her clipboard and clapping her hands. "Now you're all dressed, let's just walk through the piece. No dancing, please; no, *none*, Willow. Stand still! We need to see how you all look together on stage. It will also help you to start to get used to your costumes.

"Is everyone in position? Yes? Mrs Chang, could we have the music, please?"

The opening notes of Peter and the Wolf swirled round the room. By now, all the dancers knew them by heart. But that did not lessen their thrill.

The walk-through went well, the costumes looked lovely, and everyone was excited to be trying them on for the very first time. Getting dressed up made the end of semester show seem more real—and more urgent—somehow. But, even so, the atmosphere in the ballet school was not quite as cheerful as it had been in the weeks before previous shows. Everyone in Miss Francisco's class knew why, though no one said a word.

However, they were all thinking the same thing: "*Where was Peter?*"

In the walk–through, Miss Francisco had taken his place. But it was not the same. Not the same at all.

At that very moment, Peter was in the bath, scrubbing the mud from his knees. It was Wednesday—his first proper team soccer practice, and he'd scored a goal!

His teammates had been welcoming. Even the boy he suspected of being one of the bullies had run across the pitch to say a friendly "Hello." The team had all heard how he'd met the famous soccer players, and how he'd rescued the dog. So perhaps their friendliness wasn't for real? But so long as they stopped bullying him, Peter didn't care.

The practice session had been hard work; just as tough as ballet class, but colder, and muddier. But afterward, Peter felt wonderful. Life seemed good again.

Peter ate his dinner, watched some TV, and went to bed. He was really, really tired.

Surely he'd sleep well tonight! But then, to his surprise, he didn't. Not really. Instead, he had another ballet school dream. This time, someone had stolen all the costumes for the end of semester show. Wolf Dog, still in soccer boots, helped Peter track the thieves down. They recovered everything—except the tail for Peter's Wolf costume. There was more, much more; the dream was long and confusing. Peter still felt tired when he woke the next morning.

Back at the ballet school, Miss Francisco and Mrs Chang were huddled together in one of the offices, with Madame Olga. Although she was really old now, and had given up teaching, Madame Olga was still very much in control.

"We don't want to cancel the show," Miss Francisco was saying. She looked worried. "The other students have put so much work into it, and so have all our helpers. We don't want to disappoint them. So, if we go ahead, and if Peter isn't coming back, I think we have two choices.

"We could ask Jessamy to learn Peter's part as the Wolf, and find someone to replace her as the Cat. Jess is very good, but it wouldn't be easy, for her or her replacement. They'd both have to learn a whole new part, and how to dance with all the other soloists. And Jessamy's present part, the Cat, would be quite difficult for anyone else in the class to cope with in a hurry."

"My other idea would be to ask one of the students from the senior class to dance Peter's part as the Wolf. He—I assume we'd ask a boy; I was thinking of Alex from Grade 4—would be technically more advanced. He'd find the part fairly straightforward, but he'd still have to learn it, and do a lot of practice to be able to dance convincingly with the younger students.

If we choose Alex, he's got exams at the end of the year. Dancing in this show shouldn't interfere too much with his preparation for them, but do you think we should risk it?"

"Hmmmm," said Madam Olga, tapping her stick on the floor. "Not good! Neitherrr choice seems ideeal."

"Sally," said Mrs Chang quickly (that was Miss Francisco's first name), "Sally, have you spoken to Peter's parents again? Are they sure he won't come back?"

"Yes, I called them earlier this morning," said Miss Francisco. "And no, they're not sure. Just at the moment, Peter is very happy. Did you know he's been chosen for the school soccer team? That's boosted his confidence hugely. His mother says that, right now, all he talks about is soccer."

"And, of course," she smiled and sighed, "that business with the soccer players and the dog has encouraged him still farther.

But, considering how upset he was last Friday afternoon, I think he behaved remarkably well when he met that dog in the bushes. He's a bright and sensible boy. And a good dancer!"

"At the moment, his mother doesn't want to risk upsetting him again by talking about ballet. I think that's wise. She asks us to be patient. That's no problem for the future. I'd love to have him back in my class. The trouble is, for this end of semester show, we're running out of time!"

"Do we know why he was so unhappy last week?" asked Mrs Chang.

"No, and I don't think we should ask him," Miss Francisco replied. "Not now, anyway. If Peter wants to tell us anything in his own good time, then that's when we should be listening."

"So are we all agreed? Should I talk to Alex? Should he dance the part of the Wolf?"

"No. I say wait!" announced Madame Olga, unexpectedly. "Geeve it two or three morrre days. Then we'll see."

It was Thursday morning, very early. Peter was in bed, still trying to get the strange, jumbled images from the dream out of his mind. He felt tired and sluggish. His muscles were sore after yesterday's soccer practice, and he had a bit of a headache. He yawned, got out of bed, pattered through to the kitchen and took some milk from the refrigerator. He drank a small glassful then went back to his room. He looked at the clock on his phone; it was at least half an hour before he needed to get up and get ready for school.

He climbed back into bed, but he couldn't relax. He still felt tense and restless. Almost without thinking, he got up again, took hold of his heavy bedroom chair, and started to do his old everyday ballet exercises: Stretch, stretch, *plié, plié, relevé, relevé, battement, rond de*

jambe...

In the next room, Peter's mom was giving baby George his early morning feed. She heard the gentle "thump, thump, thump" of feet lightly tapping on the floor, and Peter's muttered counting: "One-two-three-FOUR; ONE-and-TWO-and-THREE-and-TURN..."

She smiled.

Later, when Peter came down to breakfast, she did not say anything about ballet. She simply asked him how he was. "Fine, Mom," he answered. And he meant it.

Peter and Willow both went to the same neighborhood school. Peter was a year older, and their classrooms were in different parts of the building, so they rarely saw each other. When Peter was at school, he and his classmates seemed very grown up—or that's what it felt like to Willow. They kept their distance from the younger children; especially the girls. There was nothing deliberate or unfriendly about this. It was just the way things were.

However, this Thursday, fate seemed to have arranged for things to happen differently, for a change. As he was walking through the playground on the way to his first lesson, Peter almost bumped into Willow. She came running out of a doorway; Peter could see that she was hurrying to catch up with two other girls from her class who had set off toward the library before her.

"Hey!" Peter shouted, surprised. "Look where you're going! Oh—Willow! It's you!"

"Nnnice –" he stumbled over the word, feeling suddenly awkward to be talking to her at school rather than in ballet class—"I mean, it's nice to see you!"

"Hi Peter!" said Willow. "It's good to see you too. We've all been so worried…" her voice tailed away. She didn't know how to continue. She couldn't remind Peter, here at school, that the last time she'd seen him, he'd been crying.

"We read about you and the soccer stars and their dog," she continued, changing the subject quickly. "What were they like? Was the dog really fierce…?"

Ms Simms, Willow's class teacher, walked past the pair of them.

"Willow, you should be in the library by now! Come along."

She looked at Peter, sternly. "And you. Don't you have a lesson to be going to?"

"Yes, Miss," said Peter, turning round to hurry away.

"Oh Peter!" called Willow, summoning all her courage and looking back over her shoulder. "We've missed you. We've *really* missed you."

Peter picked up his book bag and prepared

himself to face a long morning of classes about History, Geography and English.

Thursday evening was quiet—although baby George was very grizzly. "I think he's cutting another tooth," said Peter's mom. "I hope he won't keep us up all night with his crying."

Peter pulled a funny face at his baby brother, and blew a raspberry. George laughed, delighted.

"Bedtime, I think," said Peter's mom. "Sweet dreams!"

"If only!" Peter muttered to himself as he climbed upstairs. But in fact, he slept very soundly.

The next morning, over breakfast, Peter asked, "Mom! Are you busy this afternoon?"

He made a little dam of squishy cereal across a pool of milk in his bowl, then knocked it down and stirred it all together with his spoon.

"Not particularly," she answered, hiding a little flutter of excitement and relief. "Why? Is something happening?"

"Well..." said Peter. "Well, I mean... If... Perhaps..." His words seemed to be getting in a terrible muddle. He took a deep breath, turned away, and pretended to hunt for something in his book bag.

"Mom! Can you give me a lift to ballet school?"

They arrived fairly late, and Peter hoped to be able to slip into the boys' changing room unnoticed. But the girls were in the entrance hall, chatting and laughing as usual. Gloria was practicing a particularly tricky *attitude* that formed part of her Duck dance. Willow, as always, was hopping and jigging around.

Darcey was sitting on a bench, glancing at her book and joining in the conversation from time to time. Jessamy was studying a drawing she held in one hand. From a distance, Peter though that it might be a design for face paint for her Cat costume.

Attitude

"*Peeterrr!*" Willow saw him first. She rushed across the entrance hall and threw her arms around him. The other girls joined in.

"Hey!" said Peter, going red with embarrassment, "Let me breathe!"

Miss Francisco came out of the dance studio. "What's all this noise?!" She caught sight of Peter, and smiled. She hurried across the hall, and stood close beside him.

"Peter! We are so very, very pleased to see you. Welcome back. Welcome home to Rosewood Ballet School!"

The smile faded, gently, and Miss Francisco returned to her usual strict self.

"Now, everyone! Are we all ready? If anyone's not yet changed—and that means you, Peter—please hurry up! We've got a lot to do this afternoon!

The weeks had flown past. Today was the day of the end of semester performance. They'd all practiced and practiced and knew their steps perfectly. Now they'd said goodbye to their parents and brothers and sisters, and were waiting backstage, ready to change into their costumes.

Although ballet dancing seemed glamorous, the students knew that performances always involved an awful lot of most *un*glamorous hanging around. It could take over an hour for all the girls and boys to get changed into their costumes, have their hair dressed in the right style, and their faces painted in fancy patterns or covered in stage makeup. Meanwhile, all the other performers sat and read a book, or munched a snack, watched a DVD, played games on phones or tablets, or—if they were extra keen or extra nervous—did a bit of last-minute practicing.

Even so, nothing could compare, Peter said

to himself, with the feeling—and the smell—of being backstage at a theater. It was a mixture of dust and rosin and mold and paint and sawdust and makeup and (depending on which senior stars were performing) an exotic perfume or two. All this was mingled with musty upholstery, hot electrical equipment and (if he were honest) the reek of fresh and stale sweat. Peter—and many others at the ballet school—found the combination quite intoxicating.

Rosewood Ballet School didn't have a theater of its own. Instead, for important performances—even this end of semester show—Madame Olga rented a friendly old theater in a backstreet close to the city center. So there they all were, today, right now, ready to dance, anxious, excited—and waiting, waiting, waiting.

From where he stood by a window, Peter could see the orchestra arriving. The music for Peter and the Wolf did not need many players, but they had to be good. This time, the ballet school had invited senior students from the local music college to play. How smart they looked; the young women in their long dresses, the young men all wearing black—anything from a formal jacket to a baggy open-necked shirt.

It would be all right, wouldn't it? A sudden attack of nerves made Peter shake in his shoes. Quickly, he put his hand in his jacket pocket and found it—the photo of Wolf Dog that Matthias had sent to say "thank you."

On TV, Matthias had said that having Wolfie nearby always made him play better. "Well,' Peter told himself, "I will be the same! This photo will bring me luck and strength and calm. I'll take it to the theater with me. I'll be OK!'

"Peter? Are you ready?' Ruby smiled round the door of the boys' dressing room. Peter had come to the theater already dressed in thick black tights and a long-sleeved black T-shirt under his jacket. Now it was time to take that off, fasten the wolf-tail around his waist, and put on his wonderful wolf headdress. Like the tail, it was made of shaggy gray false fur fabric. It enclosed three sides of his head like a hood, and spread out downward, over his shoulders. On each side of his face, he could feel rows of plastic teeth. On top of his head, he could also feel the smooth plastic of the wolf's nose, its shiny glass eyes, and its pointy ears.

"Sit there, please, Peter," Ruby smiled at him again. "Now, try not to move or talk for the next few minutes. I'm going to make you into a big bad wolf!" Peter closed his eyes as Ruby expertly covered his face with makeup, drawing on bushy eyebrows, spiky whiskers and a lolling—blood-stained?—dark red tongue.

Everyone was ready now. Miss Francisco came into the dressing room.

"Flowers and Birds in position, please!" she called, loudly. "Curtain up in five minutes!"

Excitedly, Willow did several little hops and skips and pirouettes, knocking the book Darcey was reading out of her hands. Peter noticed that it was about wolves and dogs and foxes.

On stage, in time to the music, the Flowers had bloomed. The Birds had fluttered. The Duck had swum. The Cat had chased Willow's brilliant Bird up into the Tree. Young Peter in the story had skipped across the meadow. Old Grandfather had stepped out to enjoy the spring sunshine. Now it was time for the Wolf to appear...

Peter was ready. Carefully counting the beats, he prowled around the stage, lurking behind the dancing bushes—well done, those three hunters!—hungry for prey.

The horns snarled again. *One, two, three!* Peter sprang into the air in a wonderful series of leaps, bounding across the stage, savage, ferocious.

Teased and tormented by Willow's fluttering Bird, he crept up on Gloria's silly, innocent Duck, grabbed her by the neck, and pretended to devour her. Gloria, playing dead, arranged herself gracefully in a limp, lifeless pose on the stage.

Ballone, ballone, grand jeté. Sissonne, sissonne. And turn. Leap, leap, leap again! Peter bounded off the stage into the wings, and the audience went wild. "Bravo!" they called, clapping furiously. "What a wonderful Wolf!"

Peter didn't know it, but Matthias and Romeo were seated in the front row. His mother had told them about the performance, and they had asked her how to get tickets. "We wouldn't miss it for the world," Romeo said. Sadly, Wolfie was not allowed in the theater. But he was safe in Matthias's car outside, with a security guard watching it—and him.

Now, the orchestra played music for the final scene. In a triumphant procession, the Wolf, captured by the Hunters, was led away to the zoo.

As the whole cast danced their way across the stage, Peter slunk and snarled at the end of the rope that the Hunters had tied around his shoulders. He growled and snapped at anyone who came near—much, much more ferocious than gentle Wolf Dog had been when he was lonely and hungry and tied to the bus-shelter.

At last Peter trotted off, head lowered, tail drooping. The final curtain came down. And the applause began again.

"Cast! That was wonderful! You all danced very, very well." For once, Miss Francisco looked happy.

Still backstage, the ballet school dancers, in various stages of getting changed, wiped their sweaty faces and grinned at one another.

"Thank you, everyone, thank you!" said Miss Francisco, positively beaming with pleasure. "That really was a wonderful effort all round. And,"– she turned to where Peter was helping Ruby pack away the Wolf costume, "special thanks from us all to Peter, our lovely, leaping Wolf. We really couldn't have done it without you."

"Howwwl, Howwwlll!" said Peter, and laughed. The other dancers laughed with him.

"Now I'm part of *two* teams," he said softly to himself. "Ballet and soccer. I love them both... Howwlll! Hoowwwlll!! It's time to go home."

The end

Peter and the Wolf: The Story Behind the Ballet

The story—and the music—for *Peter and the Wolf* were written in 1936 by Russian composer Serge Prokofiev (1891–1953). He had been asked by the director of the State Children's Theater in Moscow, Russia, to create a work that would encourage very young people take an interest in music and learn to enjoy it. When writing the story, Prokofiev looked back to his own carefree childhood in the the countryside, and tried to recreate those happy feelings. He wanted to share them with his own children, and with many others.

Some people have suggested that there might also be a deeper meaning to the story of *Peter and the Wolf*. Prokofiev lived at a time when there was a harsh and strict government in Russia, his homeland. Free speech was banned. Did Prokofiev make Peter, the hero of his tale, disobedient and daring on purpose, as a way of showing —in secret code—how much he valued freedom and independence? We simply don't know.

In 1936, Prokofiev was already famous as a concert pianist and as the composer of an opera, *The Love for Three Oranges*, first performed in Chicago, USA, in 1921. The year before writing *Peter and the Wolf*, he had composed the music for one today's best-known and most dramatic ballets, *Romeo and Juliet*. It included a wonderfully strong and menacing tune, The Dance of the Knights, that has been played countles times in films and on TV, and sampled in songs by artists ranging from The Smiths and Iron Maiden to rappers and Robbie Williams.

The first official performance of *Peter and the Wolf*, in Moscow, only attracted a small audience—though a separate performance for children was a great success; they loved it. But, before long, Prokofiev's musical story became popular, first in Russia and then throughout Europe and in the USA. Today it is enjoyed worldwide, as a classic. Although not originally created as a ballet, its words and music have been interpreted by dancers ever since the 1940s, using many different styles of movement; it has been a particularly popular choice for ballet school performances. There have also been versions as films, cartoons and animations, and as stage or radio plays.

Peter and the Wolf

One morning, Peter opened the gate at the end of the garden and set off to explore the meadow beyond his Grandfather's house.

In a tree Peter saw his friend the little bird. The duck waddled after him through the open gate. She thought it would be nice to have a swim in the pond.

The duck and the bird began to argue. "What kind of bird are you if you can't fly?" said the bird.

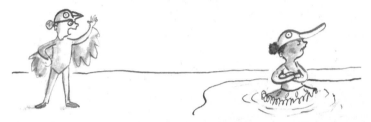

"What kind of bird are *you* if you can't swim?" replied the duck.

Suddenly, Peter noticed a cat creeping slowly through the grass.

Very quietly, the cat crept up behind the bird.

"Look out!"
shouted Peter.

The bird flew up into the
tree where it was safe.

Peter's grandfather came
outside. He was angry.
He took Peter inside.

He told him that the
meadow was dangerous
because there were
wolves around.

Just then, a big gray wolf crept out of the woods.

The wolf chased the duck... and ate it in one gulp!

Delicious!

9

The wolf waited for the cat and the bird at the base of the tree.

Peter saw what was happening. He got a strong rope...

And climbed up the tree.

He told the bird to distract the wolf.

So the bird flew around and around the wolf's head.

Meanwhile, Peter used the rope to lasso the wolf's tail.

He tied the other end of the rope to the branch.

Suddenly, some hunters returned from the woods.

Peter told them not to shoot the wolf.

They took the wolf in a joyful procession to the local zoo. Peter's grumpy grandfather brought up the rear.

And at the zoo, if you listen closely, you can still hear the duck quacking...

Because the wolf accidentally swallowed it alive!

Glossary

Attitude
Standing on one leg
with the other lifted,
usually to the front or
back. The leg in the
air is bent at the knee.

Battement tendu
Stretching one leg out
to the front or side of
the body or behind.
The toes of that leg
are pointed, but stay
on the floor.

Ecarté devant
The body is facing the
front corner and the
working leg is in the
second position.

Galop
A step for moving
quickly across the
floor. Swing one leg
forward, toe pointed,
and then jump,
bringing both feet
together in the air.
Land with your knees
gently bent (demi-
plié) and then swing
the front leg forward
again.

Galop

Pirouette

Grand jeté
A jump in which a dancer springs from one foot to land on the other with one leg forward of their body and the other stretched backward while in the air.

Pas couru
Tiny running steps.

Pas de chat
A leap from one foot to the other in which the feet are drawn up and the knees are bent.

Pas glissade
A sliding step usually used to link other steps together.

Pirouette
A full turn of the body while balancing on the toes (en pointe).

Plié
Bending the knees and then straightening them again while keeping a straight back.

Relevé
Moving from both feet flat on the floor to standing on tiptoe.

Sissone
Jumping up with both feet and "scissoring" the legs in the air before landing.

Temps lié
A movement where the legs transfer the weight of the body from one leg to the other. It can be done front, side or back.

Plié